'To read *Piranesi* is to be the labyrinth and the traveller in the labyrinth, which is poetry and prose … A novel to revisit – a house you can open again, with statues touched by quiet thoughts and strange tides'
Observer

'Clarke's imagination is prodigious, her pacing is masterly and she knows how to employ dry humour in the service of majesty'
New York Times

'Piranesi, the novel and man both, are luxuriously enigmatic and the labyrinthine House they inhabit is intoxicating. This novel is an enchanting, dark, multi-layered offering that more than lives up to the power of its predecessor' *Irish Times*

'Infinitely clever… none of [Clarke's] enchantment has worn off – it's evolved … to abide in these pages is to find oneself happily detained in awe' *Washington Post*

'It's sixteen years since *Jonathan Strange and Mr Norrell* – now Clarke is back with a new otherworldly fantasy' *Guardian*, 2020 in books

'The most gloriously peculiar book I've read in years' *Observer*

'Beautiful and bewitchingly strange' *Mail on Sunday*

'A beguiling study of isolation and exile … To say more would be to ruin one of the year's more unusual reading experiences' *i paper*, Books of the Year 2020

'Purely joyful reading' Naomi Alderman, *Spectator*, Books of the Year

'Haunting, tantalising, er⸻ ⸺l beautifully imagined fictiona⸻ ⸺ves us wondering if we are perl⸻ ⸺ing shadows for the real thing, fa⸻ ⸺ and infinite kindness within our⸻ ⸺ar

'The stuff of half-remembered dreams ... The chief joy of *Piranesi* is that it is a space with limitless room for the reader to roam through ... Clarke's novel captures the limbic fizz that comes with being alone in a place with secrets – the breathless childhood glee of unsupervised and unsanctioned exploration'
Times Literary Supplement, Books of the Year

'Sixteen long years have passed since the publication of the magnificent *Jonathan Strange & Mr Norrell*. Susanna Clarke returns at last in September with *Piranesi* ... The eerie tale of a man who lives in a flooded house' *Daily Express*

'Utterly brain-mangling ... A creepy, expertly managed crime story' *Metro*

'A book that's deliciously weird but meticulously constructed to achieve maximum suspense. Susanna Clarke doesn't just write about magic; she channels it on to the page' *Sunday Express*

'Sixteen years after *Jonathan Strange and Mr Norrell*, Susannah Clarke returns at last with the otherworldly tale of a man who lives in a flooded house' *Daily Mirror*

'A magical house with labyrinthine halls and tides that thunder up staircases' *The Times*, Autumn highlights

'The long-awaited new book from the author of *Jonathan Strange & Mr Norrell*' *Observer*

'A short and beautiful novel that reads like a poem ... in its cumulative effect of expressing an emotion and state of being that is inexpressible. It's a strange and lovely read' Buzzfeed

'Enthralling and transcendent ... Clarke's writing is clear, sharp – she can cleave your heart in a few short words ... The mystery of *Piranesi* unwinds at a tantalizing yet lightning-like pace – it's hard not to rush ahead, even when each sentence, each revelation makes you want to linger' NPR

'Plunges deep into those forbidden fortresses from which the un-mad and mortal among us are forever barred ... Clarke has un-unpicked her personality and returned to this world, our Earth, so that the rest of us might know her exquisite burden' *Wired*

'As gloriously imaginative as its predecessor ... A novel that could have been written by nobody else ... Her prose is crisp, direct and unfussy ... It's a book about the tension between those who want to possess a world and those who delight in it, describe it, honour it. It's an extraordinary book, well worth the wait' *SFX Magazine*

'Susannah Clarke's monumental masterwork *Jonathan Strange & Mr Norrell* was one of the finest works of speculative fiction of the twenty-first century and now, with *Piranesi*, she once more mines a darkly fantastical vision with a tale of a very singular house and its mysterious inhabitants. Saturated in gothic atmosphere and supernatural lore, *Piranesi* is simply unmissable' Waterstones.com

'Here is Clarke's talent in full flower; *Piranesi* is the most purely enjoyable novel I've read in a long while' *Literary Review*

'Delightful, discombobulating ... Piranesi is detective of his own existence ... Gripping' *Psychologies*

'A wonder' Slate.com

'Susanna Clarke has fashioned her own myth anew and enlarged the world again' *New Republic*

'A blend of reverie, art, mystery and the uncanny ... A beautiful, unsettling, hypnotic and, yes, singular experience' *Irish Independent*

'A novel that feels like a surreal meditation on life in quarantine' *New Yorker*

'The long-awaited followup to *Jonathan Strange* is even more magically immersive ... Here is a protagonist with no guile, no greed, no envy, no cruelty, and yet still intriguing' *Los Angeles Times*

'Why don't you trip on the new Susanna Clarke book if you want to get your mind bent but don't much care for drugs?' *New York Magazine*

'A high-quality page-turner – even the most leisurely reader will probably finish it off in a day – but its chief pleasure is immersion in its strange and uncannily attractive setting ... A standout feat' *Wall Street Journal*

'Could *Piranesi* match the hype? I'm delighted to say it has, with Clarke's singular wit and imagination still intact in a far more compressed yet still captivating tale you'll want to delve into again right after you read its sublime last sentence' *Boston Globe*

'[Piranesi's] love of the house and the meaning he finds in his humble life within it give this unusual novel a radiant, gentle, melancholy heart' *Slate*, Best Books of 2020

'Susanna Clarke's astonishing *Piranesi* proves she's one of the greatest novelists writing today' Vox

'Piranesi hit my mind and soul like a thunderbolt. It is a work of deep power' EW.com

'Spellbinding, strange, and unforgettably original' *Esquire*

'An inventive and spellbinding read' *Attitude*

'Everything about this novel is a mystery. Fantastical, very strange and not to be missed!' Alice O'Keeffe, Editor's Choice, *The Bookseller*

'An astounding, charming and challenging work. It is also – as I learned during a late-night reading – impossible to put down. It contains the foreshadowing of a well-drawn crime novel, the mystery and intrigue of Shirley Jackson's *Hill House*, and the philosophical fantasy of Philip Pullman's His Dark Materials. The world, the House and Piranesi himself will completely consume you' *Sunday Business Post*

'Okay, now everyone listen. No, I mean it, shut up for a second. We need to talk about Piranesi. I don't… I really do not know how to talk about this book beyond a very high-pitched scream and an emphatic grabbing of your knee' Tor.com

'Her prowess as a stylist is undiminished … Piranesi's naively observant voice also nods to the narrators of those Enlightenment parables of flawed Reason lost amid marvels and monsters – think Defoe's Crusoe, Swift's Gulliver, Voltaire's Candide' *Arts Desk*

'A warm book about losing and finding oneself; about what humanity could have lost in the process of becoming rational' BBC.com

'Exquisitely formed, delicately judged ... This is a novel that witnesses the limits, the transgressions, and the humanity of science. It questions what can be questioned, and reckons with the very great price of curiosity ... *Piranesi* is its own beautiful thing ... perfect in its solitude. Patient and dreadful, with a denouement so compassionately done' Lunate

'A magical mystery brilliantly voiced. Out of this world' *Saga*

'Half dream sequence, half detective story, this wonderfully playful exploration of myth and reality keeps us guessing' *The Tablet*

'I wish I could read this again for the first time. Its atmosphere of beautiful, sad loneliness is the perfect lockdown companion. There are so many things to note about the book, but here is just one: Piranesi looks with loving attention at the world in which he finds himself, caring for everything that he encounters, and receiving everything as a loving gift. Other forces, however, see it very differently. The book is deeply satisfying, with a depth of sadness – or is it joy?' *Church Times*, Books of the Year 2020

'*Piranesi* is one of those endlessly giving novels that reveal more details the more you read it, and the ending, above all, is an imperative to begin again' *Strange Horizons*

'Worth the wait. It is a haunting mystery with a winsome hero that creates a very compelling read' sfcrowsnest.info

'Unforgettable – surely one of the most original works of fiction this season. ... It's a hypnotic tale that you can devour in a day (and probably will; it's that hard to put down)' AARP

'Destined to become a work of classic fantasy' Ron Charles, CBS Sunday Morning Book Report

SUSANNA CLARKE's debut novel, *Jonathan Strange & Mr Norrell*, was longlisted for the Man Booker Prize and shortlisted for the Whitbread First Novel Award and the *Guardian* First Book Award. It won the British Book Awards Newcomer of the Year, the Hugo Award and the World Fantasy Award in 2005. Susanna Clarke is also the author of the short story collection *The Ladies of Grace Adieu*. *Piranesi* was a *Sunday Times and New York Times* bestseller, and was awarded Audies Audiobook of the Year, shortlisted for the British Book Awards Audiobook of the Year, the Costa Novel Award, the Women's Prize for Fiction, the RSL Encore Awards, the Hugo Award, the Nebula Awards, the British Science Fiction Association's Best Novel, the Bloggers Book Award; was a finalist for the Goodreads Fantasy Book of the Year, the Ray Bradbury Prize for Science Fiction and the Locus Awards; and was longlisted for the 2021 Booktube Prize. Susanna Clarke lives in Derbyshire.

PIRANESI

SUSANNA CLARKE

BLOOMSBURY PUBLISHING
LONDON · OXFORD · NEW YORK · NEW DELHI · SYDNEY

BLOOMSBURY PUBLISHING
Bloomsbury Publishing Plc
50 Bedford Square, London, WC1B 3DP, UK
29 Earlsfort Terrace, Dublin 2, Ireland

BLOOMSBURY, BLOOMSBURY PUBLISHING and the Diana logo are trademarks of
Bloomsbury Publishing Plc

First published in Great Britain 2020
This edition published 2021

A catalogue record for this book is available from the British Library

ISBN: HB: 978-1-5266-2242-6; PB: 978-1-5266-2243-3; EBOOK: 978-1-5266-2244-0;
EPDF: 978-1-5266-3410-8; WATERSTONES SPECIAL EDITION: 978-1-5266-4666-8

8 10 9 7

Typeset by Integra Software Services Pvt. Ltd.
Printed and bound in Great Britain by CPI Group (UK) Ltd, Croydon CR0 4YY

MIX
Paper from
responsible sources
FSC® C171272

To find out more about our authors and books visit www.bloomsbury.com
and sign up for our newsletters

For Colin

'I am the great scholar, the magician, the adept, who is *doing* the experiment. Of course I need subjects to do it *on*.'

The Magician's Nephew, C. S. Lewis

'People call me a philosopher or a scientist or an anthropologist. I am none of those things. I am an anamnesiologist. I study what has been forgotten. I divine what has disappeared utterly. I work with absences, with silences, with curious gaps between things. I am really more of a magician than anything else.'

Laurence Arne-Sayles, interview in
The Secret Garden, May 1976

CONTENTS

PART 1

PIRANESI

When the Moon rose in the Third Northern Hall I went to the Ninth Vestibule

ENTRY FOR THE FIRST DAY OF THE FIFTH MONTH IN THE YEAR THE ALBATROSS CAME TO THE SOUTH-WESTERN HALLS

When the Moon rose in the Third Northern Hall I went to the Ninth Vestibule to witness the joining of three Tides. This is something that happens only once every eight years.

The Ninth Vestibule is remarkable for the three great Staircases it contains. Its Walls are lined with marble Statues, hundreds upon hundreds of them, Tier upon Tier, rising into the distant heights.

I climbed up the Western Wall until I reached the Statue of a Woman carrying a Beehive, fifteen metres above the Pavement. The Woman is two or three times my own height and the Beehive is covered with marble Bees the size of my thumb. One Bee – this always gives me a slight sensation of queasiness – crawls over her left Eye. I squeezed Myself into the Woman's Niche and waited until I heard the Tides roaring in the Lower Halls and felt the Walls vibrating with the force of what was about to happen.

First came the Tide from the Far Eastern Halls. This Tide ascended the Easternmost Staircase without violence. It had no colour to speak of and its Waters were no more than ankle deep. It spread a grey mirror across the Pavement, the surface of which was marbled with streaks of milky Foam.

3

Next came the Tide from the Western Halls. This Tide thundered up the Westernmost Staircase and hit the Eastern Wall with a great Clap, making all the Statues tremble. Its Foam was the white of old fishbones, and its churning depths were pewter. Within seconds its Waters were as high as the Waists of the First Tier of Statues.

Last came the Tide from the Northern Halls. It hurled itself up the middle Staircase, filling the Vestibule with an explosion of glittering, ice-white Foam. I was drenched and blinded. When I could see again Waters were cascading down the Statues. It was then that I realised I had made a mistake in calculating the volumes of the Second and Third Tides. A towering Peak of Water swept up to where I crouched. A great Hand of Water reached out to pluck me from the Wall. I flung my arms around the Legs of the Woman carrying a Beehive and prayed to the House to protect me. The Waters covered me and for a moment I was surrounded by the strange silence that comes when the Sea sweeps over you and drowns its own sounds. I thought that I was going to die; or else that I would be swept away to Unknown Halls, far from the rush and thrum of Familiar Tides. I clung on.

Then, just as suddenly as it began, it was over. The Joined Tides swept on into the surrounding Halls. I heard the thunder and crack as the Tides struck the Walls. The Waters in the Ninth Vestibule sank rapidly down until they barely covered the Plinths of the First Tier of Statues.

I realised that I was holding on to something. I opened my hand and found a marble Finger from some Faraway Statue that the Tides had placed there.

The Beauty of the House is immeasurable; its Kindness infinite.

A description of the World
ENTRY FOR THE SEVENTH DAY OF THE FIFTH MONTH IN THE YEAR
THE ALBATROSS CAME TO THE SOUTH-WESTERN HALLS

I am determined to explore as much of the World as I can in my lifetime. To this end I have travelled as far as the Nine-Hundred-and-Sixtieth Hall to the West, the Eight-Hundred-and-Ninetieth Hall to the North and the Seven-Hundred-and-Sixty-Eighth Hall to the South. I have climbed up to the Upper Halls where Clouds move in slow procession and Statues appear suddenly out of the Mists. I have explored the Drowned Halls where the Dark Waters are carpeted with white water lilies. I have seen the Derelict Halls of the East where Ceilings, Floors – sometimes even Walls! – have collapsed and the dimness is split by shafts of grey Light.

In all these places I have stood in Doorways and looked ahead. I have never seen any indication that the World was coming to an End, but only the regular progression of Halls and Passageways into the Far Distance.

No Hall, no Vestibule, no Staircase, no Passage is without its Statues. In most Halls they cover all the available space, though here and there you will find an Empty Plinth, Niche or Apse, or even a blank space on a Wall otherwise encrusted with Statues. These Absences are as mysterious in their way as the Statues themselves.

I have observed that, while the Statues of a particular Hall are more or less uniform in size, there is considerable variation between Halls. In some places the figures are two or three times the height of a Human Being, in others more or less life-size and in yet others, only reach as high as my shoulder. The Drowned Halls contain Statues that are gigantic – fifteen to twenty metres high – but they are the exception.

I have begun a Catalogue in which I intend to record the Position, Size and Subject of each Statue, and any other points of interest. So far I have completed the First and Second South-Western Halls and am engaged on the Third. The enormity of this task sometimes makes me feel a little dizzy, but as a scientist and an explorer I have a duty to bear witness to the Splendours of the World.

The Windows of the House look out upon Great Courtyards; barren, empty places paved with stone. The Courtyards are generally four-sided, although now and then you will come upon one with six sides, or eight, or even – these are rather strange and gloomy – only three.

Outside the House there are only the Celestial Objects: Sun, Moon and Stars.

The House has three Levels. The Lower Halls are the Domain of the Tides; their Windows – when seen from across a Courtyard – are grey-green with the restless Waters and white with the spatter of Foam. The Lower Halls provide nourishment in the form of fish, crustaceans and sea vegetation.

The Upper Halls are, as I have said, the Domain of the Clouds; their Windows are grey-white and misty. Sometimes you will see a whole line of Windows suddenly illuminated by a flash of lightning. The Upper Halls give Fresh Water, which is shed in the Vestibules in the form of Rain and flows in Streams down Walls and Staircases.

Between these two (largely uninhabitable) Levels are the Middle Halls, which are the Domain of birds and of men. The Beautiful Orderliness of the House is what gives us Life.

This morning I looked out of a Window in the Eighteenth South-Eastern Hall. On the other side of the Courtyard I saw the Other looking out of a Window. The Window was tall and dark; the Other's noble head with its high forehead and neatly trimmed beard was framed in one Corner. He was lost in thought as he so often is. I waved to him. He did not see me. I waved more extravagantly. I jumped up and down with great energy. But the Windows of the House are many and he did not see me.

A list of all the people who have ever lived and what is known of them
ENTRY FOR THE TENTH DAY OF THE FIFTH MONTH IN THE YEAR THE ALBATROSS CAME TO THE SOUTH-WESTERN HALLS

Since the World began it is certain that there have existed fifteen people. Possibly there have been more; but I am a scientist and must proceed according to the evidence. Of the fifteen people whose existence is verifiable, only Myself and the Other are now living.

I will now name the fifteen people and give, where relevant, their positions.

First Person: Myself

I believe that I am between thirty and thirty-five years of age. I am approximately 1.83 metres tall and of a slender build.

Second Person: The Other

I estimate the Other's age to be between fifty and sixty. He is approximately 1.88 metres tall and, like me, of a slender build. He is strong and fit for his age. His skin is a pale olive colour. His short hair and moustache are dark brown. He has a beard that is greying, almost white; it is neatly trimmed and slightly pointed. The bones of his skull are particularly fine with high, aristocratic cheekbones and a tall, impressive forehead. The overall impression he gives is of a friendly but slightly austere person devoted to the life of the intellect.

He is a scientist like me and the only other living human being, so naturally I value his friendship highly.

The Other believes that there is a Great and Secret Knowledge hidden somewhere in the World that will grant us enormous powers once we have discovered it. What this Knowledge consists of he is not entirely sure, but at various times he has suggested that it might include the following:

1. vanquishing Death and becoming immortal
2. learning by a process of telepathy what other people are thinking
3. transforming ourselves into eagles and flying through the Air
4. transforming ourselves into fish and swimming through the Tides
5. moving objects using only our thoughts

6. snuffing out and reigniting the Sun and Stars
7. dominating lesser intellects and bending them to our will

The Other and I are searching diligently for this Knowledge. We meet twice a week (on Tuesdays and Fridays) to discuss our work. The Other organises his time meticulously and never permits our meetings to last longer than one hour.

If he requires my presence at other times, he calls out 'Piranesi!' until I come.

Piranesi. It is what he calls me.

Which is strange because as far as I remember it is not my name.

Third Person: The Biscuit-Box Man
The Biscuit-Box Man is a skeleton that resides in an Empty Niche in the Third North-Western Hall. The bones have been ordered in a particular way: long ones of a similar size have been collected and tied together with twine made from seaweed. To the right is placed the skull and to the left is a biscuit box containing all the small bones – finger bones, toe bones, vertebrae etc. The biscuit box is red. It has a picture of biscuits and bears the legend, *Huntley Palmers* and *Family Circle*.

When I first discovered the Biscuit-Box Man, the seaweed twine had dried up and fallen apart and he had become rather untidy. I made new twine from fish leather and tied up his bundles of bones again. Now he is in good order once more.

Fourth Person: The Concealed Person
One day three years ago I climbed the Staircase in the Thirteenth Vestibule. Finding that the Clouds had departed

from that Region of the Upper Halls and that they were bright, clear and filled with Sunlight, I determined to explore further. In one of the Halls (the one positioned directly above the Eighteenth North-Eastern Hall) I found a half-collapsed skeleton wedged in a narrow space between a Plinth and the Wall. From the current disposition of the bones I believe it was originally in a sitting position with the knees drawn up to the chin. I have been unable to learn the gender. If I took the bones out to examine them, I could never get them back in again.

Persons Five to Fourteen: The People of the Alcove

The People of the Alcove are all skeletal. Their bones are laid side by side on an Empty Plinth in the Northernmost Alcove of the Fourteenth South-Western Hall.

I have tentatively identified three skeletons as female and three as male, and there are four whose gender I cannot determine with any certainty. One of these I have named the Fish-Leather Man. The skeleton of the Fish-Leather Man is incomplete and many of the bones are much worn away by the Tides. Some are scarcely more than little pebbles of bone. There are small holes bored in the ends of some of them and fragments of fish leather. From this I draw several conclusions:

1. The skeleton of the Fish-Leather Man is older than the others
2. The skeleton of the Fish-Leather Man was once displayed differently, its bones threaded together with thongs of fish leather, but over time the leather decayed

3. The people who came after the Fish-Leather Man (presumably the People of the Alcove) held human life in such reverence that they patiently collected his bones and laid him with their own dead

Question: when I feel myself about to die, ought I to go and lie down with the People of the Alcove? There is, I estimate, space for four more adults. Though I am a young man and the day of my Death is (I hope) some way off, I have given this matter some thought.

Another skeleton lies next to the People of the Alcove (though this does not count as one of the people who have lived). It is the remains of a creature approximately 50 centimetres long and with a tail the same length as its body. I have compared the bones to the different kinds of Creatures that are portrayed in the Statues and believe them to belong to a monkey. I have never seen a live monkey in the House.

The Fifteenth Person: The Folded-Up Child
The Folded-Up Child is a skeleton. I believe it to be female and approximately seven years of age. She is posed on an Empty Plinth in the Sixth South-Eastern Hall. Her knees are drawn up to her chin, her arms clasp her knees, her head is bowed down. There is a necklace of coral beads and fishbones around her neck.

I have given a great deal of thought to this child's relationship to me. There are living in the World (as I have already explained) only Myself and the Other; and we are both male. How will the World have an Inhabitant when we are dead? It is my belief that the World (or, if you will, the House, since the two are for all practical purposes identical) wishes an Inhabitant for Itself to be a witness to its Beauty and the recipient of its Mercies. I have postulated that the House intended the Folded-Up Child to be my Wife, only something happened to prevent it. Ever since I had this thought it has seemed only right to share with her what I have.

I visit all the Dead, but particularly the Folded-Up Child. I bring them food, water and water lilies from the Drowned Halls. I speak to them, telling them what I have been doing and I describe any Wonders that I have seen in the House. In this way they know that they are not alone.

Only I do this. The Other does not. As far as I know he has no religious practices.

The Sixteenth Person

And You. Who are You? Who is it that I am writing for? Are You a traveller who has cheated Tides and crossed Broken Floors and Derelict Stairs to reach these Halls? Or are You perhaps someone who inhabits my own Halls long after I am dead?

My Journals

ENTRY FOR THE SEVENTEENTH DAY OF THE FIFTH MONTH IN THE YEAR THE ALBATROSS CAME TO THE SOUTH-WESTERN HALLS

I write down what I observe in my notebooks. I do this for two reasons. The first is that Writing inculcates habits of precision and carefulness. The second is to preserve whatever knowledge I possess for you, the Sixteenth Person. I keep my notebooks in a brown leather messenger bag; the bag is generally stored in a hollow place behind the Statue of an Angel caught on a Rose Bush in the North-Eastern Corner of the Second Northern Hall. This is also where I keep my watch, which I need on Tuesdays and Fridays when I go to meet the Other at 10 o'clock. (On other days I try not to carry my watch for fear that Sea Water will get inside and damage the mechanism.)

One of my notebooks is my Table of Tides. In it I set down the Times and Volumes of High and Low Tides and make calculations of the Tides to come. Another notebook is my Catalogue of Statues. In the others I keep my Journal in which I write my thoughts and memories and make a record of my days. So far my Journal has filled nine notebooks; this is the tenth. All are numbered and most are labelled with the dates to which they refer.

No. 1 is labelled *December 2011 to June 2012*

No. 2 is labelled *June 2012 to November 2012*

No. 3 was originally labelled *November 2012*, but this has been crossed out at some point and relabelled *Thirtieth Day in the Twelfth Month in the Year of Weeping and Wailing, to the Fourth Day of the Seventh Month in the Year I discovered the Coral Halls*

Both No. 2 and No. 3 have gaps where pages have been violently removed. I have puzzled over the reason for this and tried to imagine who might have done it, but as yet have reached no conclusion.

No. 4 is labelled *Tenth Day of the Seventh Month in the Year I discovered the Coral Halls, to the Ninth Day of the Fourth Month in the Year I named the Constellations*

No. 5 is labelled *Fifteenth Day of the Fourth Month in the Year I named the Constellations, to the Thirtieth Day of the Ninth Month in the Year I counted and named the Dead*

No. 6 is labelled *First Day of the Tenth Month in the Year I counted and named the Dead, to the Fourteenth Day of the Second Month in the Year that the Ceilings in the Twentieth and Twenty-First North-Eastern Halls collapsed*

No. 7 is labelled *Seventeenth Day of the Second Month in the Year that the Ceilings in the Twentieth and Twenty-First North-Eastern Halls collapsed, to the last Day of the same Year*

No. 8 is labelled *First Day of the Year I travelled to the Nine-Hundred-and-Sixtieth Western Hall, to the Fifteenth Day of the Tenth Month of the same Year*

No. 9 is labelled *Sixteenth Day of the Tenth Month in the Year I travelled to the Nine-Hundred-and-Sixtieth Western Hall, to the Fourth Day of the Fifth Month in the Year the Albatross came to the South-Western Halls*

This Journal (No. 10) was begun on the Fifth Day of the Fifth Month in the Year the Albatross came to the South-Western Halls.

One of the drawbacks of keeping a journal is the difficulty of finding important entries again and so it is my practice to use one notebook as an index to all the others. In this notebook I have allocated a certain number of pages to each letter of the alphabet (more pages for common letters, such as A and C; fewer for letters that occur less frequently, for example Q and X). Under each letter I list entries by subject and where in my Journals they are to be found.

Reading over what I have just written, I have realised something. I have used two systems to number the years. How could I not have noticed this before?

I am guilty of bad practice. Only one system of numbering is needed. Two introduces confusion, uncertainty, doubt and muddle. (And is aesthetically unpleasing.)

In accordance with the first system I have named two years 2011 and 2012. This strikes me as deeply pedestrian. Also I cannot remember what happened two thousand years ago which made me think that year a good starting point. According to the second system I have given the years names like 'The Year I named the Constellations' and 'The Year I counted and named the Dead'. I like this much more. It gives each year a character of its own. This is the system I shall use going forward.

Statues
ENTRY FOR THE EIGHTEENTH DAY OF THE FIFTH MONTH IN THE YEAR THE ALBATROSS CAME TO THE SOUTH-WESTERN HALLS

There are some Statues that I love more than the rest. The Woman carrying a Beehive is one.

Another – perhaps *the* Statue that I love above all others – stands at a Door between the Fifth and Fourth North-Western Halls. It is the Statue of a Faun, a creature half-man and half-goat, with a head of exuberant curls. He smiles slightly and presses his forefinger to his lips. I have always felt that he meant to tell me something or perhaps to warn me of something:

Quiet! he seems to say. *Be careful!* But what danger there could possibly be I have never known. I dreamt of him once; he was standing in a snowy forest and speaking to a female child.

The Statue of a Gorilla that stands in the Fifth Northern Hall always catches my eye. He is depicted squatting on his Lower Limbs, leaning forward and propping himself up on his Powerful Arms and Fists. His Face fascinates me. His Great Brow overshadows his Eyes and in a human person this expression would be called a scowl, but in the Gorilla it seems to mean the exact opposite. He represents many things, among them Peace, Tranquillity, Strength and Endurance.

There are many others that I love – the Young Boy playing the Cymbals, the Elephant carrying a Castle, the Two Kings playing Chess. The last I will mention is not exactly a favourite. Rather it is a Statue, or, to be more exact, a pair of Statues, that never fails to arrest my attention whenever I see it. The two Statues flank the Eastern Door of the First Western Hall. They are approximately six metres tall and have two unusual features: firstly, they are much larger than the other Statues in the First Western Hall; secondly, they are incomplete. Their Trunks emerge from the Wall at their Waists; their Arms reach back to push mightily; their Muscles swell with the effort and their Faces are contorted. They are not comfortable to contemplate. They seem to be in pain, struggling to be born; the struggle may be fruitless and yet they do not give up. Their Heads are extravagantly horned and so I have named them the Horned Giants. They represent Endeavour and the Struggle against a Wretched Fate.

Is it disrespectful to the House to love some Statues more than others? I sometimes ask Myself this question. It is my belief that the House itself loves and blesses equally everything that it has created. Should I try to do the same? Yet, at the same time, I can see that it is in the nature of men to prefer one thing to another, to find one thing more meaningful than another.

Do trees exist?

ENTRY FOR THE NINETEENTH DAY OF THE FIFTH MONTH IN THE YEAR THE ALBATROSS CAME TO THE SOUTH-WESTERN HALLS

Many things are unknown. Once – it was about six or seven months ago – I saw a bright yellow speck floating on a gentle Tide beneath the Fourth Western Hall. Not understanding what it could be, I waded out into the Waters and caught it. It was a leaf, very beautiful, with two sides curving to a point at each end. Of course it is possible that it was part of a type of sea vegetation that I have never seen, but I am doubtful. The texture seemed wrong. Its surface repelled Water, like something meant to live in Air.

PART 2

THE OTHER

Batter-Sea

This morning at ten o'clock I went to the Second South-
Western Hall to meet the Other. When I entered the Hall he
was already there, leaning on an Empty Plinth, tapping at one
of his shining devices. He wore a well-cut suit of charcoal wool
and a bright white shirt that contrasted pleasingly with the
olive tones of his skin.

Without looking up from his device he said, 'I need some
data.'

He is often like this: so intent on what he is doing that he
forgets to say Hello or Goodbye or to ask me how I am. I do
not mind. I admire his dedication to his scientific work.

'What data?' I asked. 'Can I assist you?'

'Certainly,' he said. 'In fact, I won't get far if you don't.
Today the subject of my research is' – at this point he looked
up from what he was doing and smiled at me – 'you.' He has a
most charming smile when he remembers to use it.

'Really?' I said. 'What are you trying to find out? Do you
have a hypothesis about me?'

'I do.'

'What is it?'

'I can't tell you that. It might influence the data.'

'Oh! Yes. That is true. Sorry.'

'That's OK,' he said. 'It's natural to be curious.' He placed his shining device on the Empty Plinth and turned around. 'Sit down,' he said.

I sat on the Pavement, cross-legged, and waited for his questions.

'Comfortable?' he said. 'Good. Now tell me. What do you remember?'

'What do I remember?' I asked, confused.

'Yes.'

'As a question it lacks specificity,' I said.

'Nevertheless,' he said. 'Try to answer it.'

'Well,' I said. 'I suppose the answer is everything. I remember everything.'

'Really?' he said. 'That's rather a large claim. Are you sure?'

'I think so.'

'Give me some examples of the things you remember.'

'Well,' I said, 'suppose you were to name a Hall many days journey from here. Providing that I had visited it before, I could immediately tell you how to get there. I could name every Hall you would need to travel through. I could describe the notable Statues you would see on the Walls, and, with a reasonable degree of accuracy, I could tell you their positions – which Wall they stood against, whether North, South, East or West – and how far along the Wall they stood. I could also enumerate all the ... '

'What about Batter-Sea?' asked the Other.

'Um ... What?'

'Batter-Sea. Do you remember Batter-Sea?'

'No ... I ... Batter-Sea?'

'Yes.'

'I do not understand … '

I waited for the Other to explain, but he said nothing. I could see that he was observing me closely and I was sure that this question was crucial to whatever research he was conducting, but as to how I was supposed to answer it, I had not the least idea.

'Batter-Sea is not a word,' I said at last. 'It has no referent. There is nothing in the World corresponding to that combination of sounds.'

Still the Other said nothing. He continued to gaze at me intently. I gazed back, troubled.

Then: 'Oh!' I exclaimed, light suddenly dawning. 'I see what you are doing!' I started to laugh.

'What am I doing?' asked the Other, smiling.

'You need to find out if I am telling the truth. I just said that I can describe the way to any Hall that I have previously visited. But you have no way of judging the truth of my claim. For example, if I were to describe the Path to the Ninety-Sixth Northern Hall, you would not know if my directions were accurate because you have never been there. So you have asked me a question with a nonsense word in it – Batter-Sea. Very cunningly you have chosen a word that sounds like a place. A place that is battered by the Sea. Now if I were to say that I remembered Batter-Sea and then described the way there, you would know I was lying. You would know I was simply boasting. You have put this in as a control question.'

'That's it exactly,' he said. 'That's exactly what I am doing.'

We both laughed.

'Have you more questions for me?' I asked.

'No. All done.' He was about to turn away to enter the data in his shining device, but something about me caught his attention and he gave me a puzzled sort of look.

'What is it?' I asked.

'Your glasses. What happened to them?'

'My glasses?'

'Yes,' he said. 'They look slightly … odd.'

'What do you mean?'

'The arms are wrapped round and round with strips of something,' he said. 'And the ends hang down at the sides.'

'Oh! I see,' I said. 'Yes! The arms of my glasses keep breaking off. First the left. And then the right. The salt-laden Air corrodes the plastic. I am experimenting with different methods of mending them. On the left arm I have used strips of fish leather and fish glue and on the right arm I have used seaweed. That is less successful.'

'Yes,' he said. 'I imagine it would be.'

In the Halls beneath us the incoming Tide struck a Wall. *Boom.* It withdrew, surged forward through the Doors and struck the Wall of the Next Chamber. *Boom. Boom. Boom.* Withdrew again; surged forward again. *Boom.* The Second South-Western Hall thrummed like the plucked string of an instrument.

The Other looked anxious. 'That sounded really close,' he said. 'Oughtn't we to be getting out of here?' He does not understand the Tides.

'There is no need,' I said.

'OK,' he said. But he was not reassured. His eyes widened and his breathing became more shallow and rapid. He kept glancing from Door to Door as though expecting to see Water pouring in at any second.

'I don't want to get caught,' he said.

Once the Other was in the Eighth Northern Hall. A strong Tide from the Northern Halls rose in the Tenth Vestibule, followed moments later by an equally strong Tide from the Eastern Halls in the Twelfth Vestibule. Vast quantities of Water poured into the surrounding Halls, including the one where the Other was. The Waters plucked him up and carried him away, sweeping him through Doors and battering him against Walls and Statues. Several times he was completely immersed, and he expected to drown. Eventually the Tides cast him up on the Pavement of the Third Western Hall (a distance of seven Halls from where he began). That is where I found him. I fetched him a blanket and hot soup made of seaweed and mussels. As soon as he was able to walk, he took himself off without a word. I do not know where he went. (I never really know.) This happened in the Sixth Month of the Year I named the Constellations. Since then the Other has been afraid of the Tides.

'There is no danger,' I told him.

'Are you sure?' he said.

Boom. Boom.

'Yes,' I said. 'In five minutes, the Tide will reach the Sixth Vestibule and mount the Staircase. The Second Southern Hall – two Halls east of here – will be flooded for an hour. But the

Water will be no more than ankle deep and it will not reach us.'

He nodded, but his anxiety levels remained high and he left a short while after.

In the early evening I went to the Eighth Vestibule to fish. I was not thinking about my conversation with the Other; I was thinking of my supper and of the beauty of the Statues in the Evening Light. But as I stood, casting my net into the Waters of the Lower Staircase, an image rose up before me. I saw a black scribble against a grey Sky and a flicker of bright red; words drifted towards me – white words on a black background. At the same time, there was a sudden blare of noise and a metallic taste on my tongue. And all of the images – no more than fragments or ghosts of images really – seemed to coalesce around the strange word, 'Batter-Sea'. I tried to get hold of them, to bring them into sharper focus, but like a dream they faded and were gone.

A white cross
ENTRY FOR THE THIRTIETH DAY OF THE FIFTH MONTH IN THE YEAR THE ALBATROSS CAME TO THE SOUTH-WESTERN HALLS

If you examine my previous Journal (Journal no. 9) you will see that I wrote very little in the final month of last year and the first month and a half of this one. (This sometimes happens for a reason that I will explain below.) During this period an event took place, which I have been meaning to write about. I shall do so now.

It was the very depths of Winter. Snow was piled on the Steps of the Staircases. Every Statue in the Vestibules wore a cloak or shroud or hat of snow. Every Statue with an outstretched Arm (of which there are many) held an icicle like a dangling sword or else a line of icicles hung from the Arm as if it were sprouting feathers.

There is a thing that I know but always forget: Winter is hard. The cold goes on and on and it is only with difficulty and effort that a person keeps himself warm. Every year, as Winter approaches, I congratulate Myself on having a plentiful supply of dry seaweed to use as fuel, but as the days, weeks and months stretch out I become less certain that I have sufficient. I wear as many of my clothes as I can cram onto my body. Every Friday I take stock of my fuel and I calculate how much I can permit Myself each day in order to make it last until Spring.

In the Twelfth Month of last year the Other suspended his work on the Great and Secret Knowledge and cancelled our meetings because he said it was too cold to stand about talking. My fingers were numb with cold – which caused my hand-writing to deteriorate. Eventually I stopped writing in my Journal altogether.

About the middle of the First Month a Wind came up from the South. It blew for days without ceasing and though I tried hard not to complain about it, I found it something of a trial. It blew stinging Snow into the Halls. It blew on me at night in my bed in the Third Northern Hall. It howled in the Vestibules, catching up handfuls of loose snow and making them into little ghosts.

Not everything about the Wind was bad. Sometimes it blew through the little voids and crevices of the Statues and caused them to sing and whistle in surprising ways; I had never known the Statues to have voices before and it made me laugh for sheer delight.

One day I rose early and went to the Forty-Third Vestibule. The Halls that I passed through were grey and dim, with just a suggestion of Light in the Windows – the idea of Light, more than Light itself.

My intention was to gather seaweed, both for food and fuel. Normally I must wait until Spring, Summer and Autumn to dry seaweed. Winter is too cold and wet. But it had occurred to me that if I could hang the seaweed up (perhaps across a Doorway) then the Wind would dry it quickly. The only difficulty would be in securing the seaweed so that it did not blow away. I had thought of three different ways to do this and was eager to try all of them to see which would prove the most efficient.

As I crossed the Eleventh Western Hall, the Wind knocked me from one Paving Stone to another as if I were a chess piece on a board. (I made some highly original moves!)

I descended the Staircase in the Forty-Third Vestibule and entered the Lower Hall, the one that lies directly beneath the Thirty-Seventh South-Western Hall. One effect of the Wind was that the High Tides were much higher and more violent than usual; the Low Tides were conversely lower. It was Low Tide just then and the Sea had drawn back so far that the Hall was entirely empty of Water (which hardly ever happens). It was strewn with remnants of the Tide: seaweed, which streamed in the Wind like little banners, and pebbles, starfish and shells, which rattled across the Stone Pavement as the Wind chased them.

It was early, a handful of moments after Dawn. I could see the pale golden Sky reflected in some of the Windows in the Courtyard. Ahead of me the grey, restless Waters were framed in the Doorway that led to the next Hall. The wildness of the Water contrasted with the severity of the lines of the Doorway.

I bent down and began to gather the cold, wet seaweed. Even this simple task was made more difficult by the Wind, since so much of my energy had to be expended on staying in the same place. The Wind also caught the strands of seaweed; they lashed my hands and made them cold and sore.

After a while I straightened Myself to ease my back. Once again, I raised my eyes to the Doorway that led to the next Hall.

I saw a vision! In the dim Air above the grey Waves hung a white, shining cross. Its whiteness was a blazing whiteness; it far outshone the Wall of Statues behind it. It was beautiful but I did not understand it. The next moment brought enlightenment of a sort: it was not a cross at all but something vast and white, which glided rapidly towards me on the Wind.

What could it be? It must be a bird, but if I could see it at such a great distance, then it must be a bird of much greater size than the birds I was accustomed to. It swept on, coming directly towards me. I spread my arms in answer to its spread wings, as if I was going to embrace it. I spoke out loud. *Welcome! Welcome! Welcome!* was what I think I meant to say, but the Wind took my breath from me and all I could manage was: 'Come! Come! Come!'

The bird sailed across the heaving Waves, never once beating its wings. With great skill and ease it tipped itself slightly sideways to pass through the Doorway that separated us. Its wingspan surpassed even the width of the Door. I knew what it was! An albatross!

Still it continued, straight towards me, and the strangest thought came to me: perhaps the albatross and I were destined to merge and the two of us would become another order of being entirely: an Angel! This thought both excited and frightened me, but still I remained, arms outstretched, mirroring the albatross's flight. (I thought how surprised the Other would be when I flew into the Second South-Western Hall on my Angel Wings, bringing him messages of Peace and Joy!) My heart beat rapidly.

The moment that he reached me – the moment that I thought we would collide like Planets and become one! – I gave out a sort of gasping cry – *Aahhhh!* In the same instant, I felt some sort of pent-up tension go out of me, a tension I did not know I had until that moment. Vast, white wings passed over me. I felt and smelt the Air those wings brought with them, the sharp, salty, wild tang of Faraway Tides and Winds that had roamed vast distances, through Halls I would never see.

At the last moment the albatross swung over my left shoulder. I fell to the Pavement. He flapped his wings in a frantic, panicked sort of way, stuck out his wiry pink legs and tumbled out of the Air into a sort of heap on the Pavement. In the Air he was a miraculous being – a Heavenly Being – but on the Stones of the Pavement he was mortal and subject to the same embarrassments and clumsiness as other mortals.

We picked ourselves up. Now that he was on the dry Pavement he seemed bigger than ever: his head reached almost to my breastbone.

'I am very glad to see you,' I said. 'Welcome. I am the Inhabitant of these Halls. One of the Inhabitants. There is another, but he is not fond of birds and so you will probably not see him.'

The albatross spread his wings wide and stretched out his throat towards the Ceiling. He made a sort of clacking, whirring sound in his throat, which I took to be his way of greeting me. The backs of his wings were dark, almost black, with a white shape like a star on each one.

I returned to my work of gathering seaweed. The albatross walked about the Hall. His greyish-pinkish feet made loud slapping sounds on the Pavement. From time to time he came and looked at what I was doing as if it interested him.

The next day I returned. The albatross had come up the Staircase and was examining the Forty-Third Vestibule. But more than that: imagine my joy when I found that the Vestibule now sheltered two albatrosses! His wife had joined him! (Or perhaps the original albatross was female and this was her husband. I did not have enough information to be certain on this point.) The new albatross had a different patterning on the back of her (or possibly his) wings: a patterning of white flecks, like a silver rain falling. The two albatrosses spread their wings; they danced around each other; they pointed their beaks at the Ceiling and made a joyful shrieking, screeching sound; they tapped their long pink beaks together to express their happiness.

A few days later I visited them again. This time they seemed quieter and there was an air of despondency and discouragement in the Vestibule. The albatross that I thought of as male (the one with stars on his wings) had fetched up a quantity of seaweed from the Lower Hall. He picked up lumps of it in his beak and made a heap of them. A few minutes later he became dissatisfied with this arrangement and collected the lumps of seaweed again and tried them in a different spot. He performed this action perhaps a dozen times.

'I think I see your problem,' I said. 'You have come here to build a nest. But you cannot find the materials you need. There is only cold, wet seaweed and you need something drier to make a cosy nest for your egg. Do not worry. I will help you. I have a supply of dry seaweed. Speaking as a non-avian, I feel sure that this would be a highly suitable building material. I will go and fetch it immediately.'

The starred albatross spread his wings and stretched his neck; he pointed his beak at the Ceiling and made the raucous clacking sound. This, I thought, was an expression of enthusiasm.

I returned to the Third Northern Hall. I lined a fishing net with heavy-gauge plastic. Inside I placed what I thought was the right amount of nesting material for two such enormous birds. It approximated to three days' fuel. This was no insignificant amount and I knew that I might be colder because I had given it away. But what is a few days of feeling cold compared to a new albatross in the World? I made two other additions to the pile of seaweed: some clean, white feathers that I had found and kept for no better reason than because I liked them, and an old woollen jumper that was in so many holes it was of scarcely any use as a garment, but which might do very well as a lining for a precious egg.

I dragged the fishing net to the Forty-Third Vestibule. I was immediately rewarded by the interest which the male albatross showed in the contents; he seized a beakful of dry seaweed and began trying it out in different places.

Shortly thereafter the albatrosses built a tall nest approximately a metre wide at its base and laid an egg in it. They are excellent parents; they were devoted to their egg and are now equally diligent in caring for their chick. The chick grows slowly and has shown no sign of being ready to fledge.

I have named this year the Year the Albatross came to the South-Western Halls.

The birds sit silent in the Sixth Western Hall
ENTRY FOR THE THIRTY-FIRST DAY OF THE FIFTH MONTH IN THE YEAR THE ALBATROSS CAME TO THE SOUTH-WESTERN HALLS

Ever since the Ceilings of the Twentieth and Twenty-First North-Eastern Halls collapsed two years ago, the Weather in this Region of the House has changed. Clouds drift down through the Broken Ceilings and into the Middle Halls where normally they would not go. It makes the World chill and grey.

This morning I awoke cold and shivering. A Cloud had penetrated the Third Northern Hall where I sleep. The Statues were delicate white images painted on white Mist.

I rose quickly and busied Myself with my daily tasks. I gathered seaweed in the Ninth Vestibule and made Myself a breakfast of nourishing, warming soup; then I set off for the Third South-Western Hall to continue my work on the Catalogue of Statues.

The House was peculiarly silent. No birds flew; no birds sang. Where had they all gone? It seemed they found the Cloud-haunted World as oppressive as I did. In the Sixth Western Hall I found them at last. They were gathered there, perched on the Shoulders and Heads of every Statue, on Plinths and on Columns, sitting silently, waiting.

The Drowned Halls
ENTRY FOR THE EIGHTH DAY OF THE SIXTH MONTH IN THE YEAR THE ALBATROSS CAME TO THE SOUTH-WESTERN HALLS

East of the First Vestibule the House is Derelict. Masonry and Statues from the Upper Halls have fallen through Broken Floors into the Middle and Lower Halls, blocking Doorways. There is an Area covering perhaps as many as forty or fifty Halls where the Tides cannot penetrate. Over time the Sea Water has drained away and these Halls have filled up with Rain, making dark, still, freshwater Lakes. Their Windows are half-sub-merged in Water or blocked by Masonry, making them dim and shadowy. Cut off from the Tides, they are unusually silent.

These are the Drowned Halls.

On the Periphery of this Region the Waters are shallow, tranquil and covered with water lilies, but in the centre they are deep and treacherous, full of broken Masonry and drowned Statues. The majority of the Drowned Halls are inaccessible, but some can be entered from the Upper Level.

They contain giant Statues of Men with curly Heads and Beards that strain and struggle out of the confines of the Walls, extending their Upper Bodies over the Dark Waters. There is one in particular who leans out so far that his broad, muscular Back forms an almost horizontal platform half a metre or so above the level of the Water, making an excellent place from which to fish.

Night fishing is best, when the fish are drawn to play in spots of bright Moonlight and are easy to see.

The Clouds above the Nineteenth Eastern Hall
ENTRY FOR THE TENTH DAY OF THE SIXTH MONTH IN THE YEAR THE ALBATROSS CAME TO THE SOUTH-WESTERN HALLS

It used to be that I dared not live too close to the Tides. When I heard their Thunder, I ran and hid Myself. In my ignorance, I feared to be caught in their Waters and drowned.

As far as possible I kept to the Dry Halls where the Statues are not clothed in rags of seaweed or armoured with encrustations of shellfish, where the Air is not scented with the Tides: Halls, in other words, that have not been flooded in recent Times. Water was not a problem; most Halls contain Falls of Fresh Water (sometimes you will see a Statue almost bisected by the Water that has splashed onto it for centuries). Food was a different matter; for that I had to brave the Tides. I would go to the Vestibules and descend the Staircases to the Lower Halls, to the Rim of the Ocean. But the Force of the Waves frightened me.

Even then I knew that the Tides were not random. I saw that if I could record and document them, I might be able to predict their appearance. That was the beginning of my Table. But, though I grasped certain things about the movements of the Tides, I had no understanding of their Natures. I thought one Tide was pretty much the same as all the others. It astonished me when I went to meet a Tide expecting plentiful fish and sea vegetation, only to find it bright, clean, empty.

I was often hungry.

Fear and hunger forced me to explore the House and I discovered that fish were plentiful in the Drowned Halls. Their Waters were still and I was not so afraid. The difficulty here was that the Drowned Halls were surrounded by Dereliction on all sides. To reach them it was necessary to go up to the Upper Halls and then descend by means of the Wreckage through the great Rents and Gashes in the Floor.

Once, when I had not eaten for two days, I determined to go to the Drowned Halls to find some food. I ascended to the Upper Halls. This in itself was not easy for someone in my enfeebled condition. The Staircases, though they vary in size, are mostly built on the same noble scale as the rest of the House and each Step is almost twice the height that is comfortable for me. (It is as though God had originally built the House intending to people it with Giants before inexplicably changing His Mind.)

I passed into one of the Upper Halls, the one that stands directly above the Nineteenth Eastern Hall. From there I intended to descend to the Drowned Halls, but to my dismay I found that the Hall was full of Clouds: a chill, grey, wet blank.

I had my Journal with me. Consulting it, I discovered that I had been in this Vicinity once before and had in fact made detailed notes of the Hall beyond this one; the Hall above the Twentieth Eastern Hall. I had described the character and condition of the Statues and had even made a sketch of one of them. But of this Hall – the Hall on whose Threshold I now stood, the Hall that was full of Clouds – of this Hall I had recorded nothing whatsoever.

Today I would consider it madness to journey through a Hall I cannot see properly and of which I have no record, but today I do not allow Myself to get as hungry as I was then.

Adjoining Halls usually share some characteristics. The Hall immediately to my rear was approximately 200 metres in length and 120 metres wide and so the chances were good that the Hall before me was the same. It did not seem an impossible distance; I was more concerned about the Statues. From what I could see, these depicted Human or Demi-Human figures, all two or three times my own stature and all in the throes of violent action: Men fighting, Women and Men being carried off by Centaurs or Satyrs, Octopuses tearing People apart. In most Regions of the House the expressions of the Statues are joyful or tranquil or possessed of a distant calm; but here the Faces were distorted in screams of rage or anguish.

I resolved to go carefully. To bash oneself on an outstretched marble limb is painful.

I entered the Cloud and slowly made my way along the Northern Side of the Hall. Statues appeared, one by one, out of the pale Cloud. They covered the Walls so thickly and were twisted into such tortuous forms that it was like walking under the dripping branches of a great forest of Arms and Bodies.

One Statue had toppled from the Wall and was lying shattered on the Floor. This ought to have been a warning to me.

I came to a place where a Statue thrust itself a long way out from the Wall. It depicted a Man, his vast Body flailing backwards, stretched over the Pavement, his Arms thrown over his Head as a Centaur trampled on him. The Palms of his great Hands faced upwards and his Fingers were curled in agony. I took a step away from the Wall to circumvent him and my foot met with …

… nothing.

No Floor! No Stone Pavement beneath me! I was falling! I lunged in terror towards the Wall. Immediately, I was caught! I lay suspended over the Empty Air, too terrified to move, my mind deadened by fear and shock. By some miracle I had fallen into the Trampled Man's Hands. The Hands were dripping with wet and horribly slippery; any movement on my part threatened to loose his hold on me and send me tumbling into the Void. Whimpering with fear and clinging to the Trampled Man with every atom of my strength, I inched up his Arms to his Head; from his Head to his Chest and so to his Lap where I wedged myself in. The Body of the Attacking Centaur formed a sort of Ceiling two or three centimetres over my head. The Cloud was so dense that I could not see where the Floor began again.

I stayed there all day and all night, hungry, almost dead from cold but deeply grateful to the Trampled Man for saving me. In the morning the Wind came and carried the Cloud westwards. I peered out at the great Gash in the Floor and I saw the dizzying drop – 30 metres or more – to the still Waters of the Drowned Hall beneath.

A conversation

As well as my regular meetings with the Other and the quiet, consolatory presence of the Dead, there are the birds. Birds are not difficult to understand. Their behaviour tells me what they are thinking. Generally it runs along the lines of: *Is this food? Is this? What about this? This might be food. I am almost certain that this is.* Or occasionally: *It is raining. I do not like it.*

While ample for a brief neighbourly exchange, such remarks do not suggest a broad or deep intelligence. Yet it has occurred to me that there may be more wisdom in birds than appears at first sight, a wisdom that reveals itself only obliquely and intermittently.

Once – it was an evening in Autumn – I came to the Doorway of the Twelfth South-Eastern Hall intending to pass through the Seventeenth Vestibule. I found that I was unable to enter it; the Vestibule was full of birds and the birds were all aflight. They circled and spiralled, creating a whirling dance. They filled the Vestibule like a column of smoke, which grew darker and denser in places and the next moment lighter and airier. I have witnessed this dance on several occasions, always in the evening and in the later months of the year.

Another time I entered the Ninth Vestibule and found it full of little birds. They were of different kinds, but mostly sparrows. I had not taken more than a few steps into the Vestibule when a large group of them took to the Air. They flew together in one great swoop up to the Eastern Wall, then in another swoop to the Southern Wall and then they turned and flew around me in a loose spiral.

'Good morning,' I said. 'I hope that you are well?'

Most of the birds scattered to different perches, but a handful – maybe as many as ten – flew to the Statue of a Gardener in the North-West Corner. They remained there for perhaps thirty seconds and then, still together, they ascended to a higher Statue on the Western Wall: the Woman carrying a Beehive. The birds remained on the Statue of the Woman carrying a Beehive for a minute or so and then they flew away.

I wondered why out of the thousand or so Statues in the Vestibule the little birds had chosen these two to perch on. It occurred to me – it was no more than an idle thought – that both these Statues might be said to represent Industriousness. The Gardener is old and bent, and yet he digs faithfully in his garden. The Woman is pursuing her profession of beekeeping and the Beehive that she carries is full of bees who are also patiently carrying out their tasks. Were the birds telling me that I ought to be industrious too? That seemed unlikely. After all I was already industrious! I was at that very moment on my way to the Eighth Vestibule to fish. I carried fishing nets over my shoulder and a lobster trap made from an old bucket.

The warning of the birds – if that was what it was – seemed on the face of it nonsensical, but I decided nonetheless to follow this unusual line of reasoning and see where it took me. That day I caught seven fish and four lobsters. I threw none of them back.

That night a Wind came from the West, bringing an unexpected Storm. The Tides were made turbulent and the fish were driven away from their customary Halls far out to Sea. For the next two days there were no fish at all and if I had not attended to the birds' warning I would have had hardly anything to eat.

This experience led me to form a hypothesis: perhaps the wisdom of birds resides, not in the individual, but in the flock, the congregation. I have tried to think of an experiment that would test this theory. The problem, as I see it, is that it is impossible to know in advance when such events will occur; and so the only viable course of action is months – more likely years – of careful observation and meticulous record keeping. Unfortunately, this is not possible just now since so much of my time is taken up by my work with the Other (I refer of course to our search for the Great and Secret Knowledge).

However, it is with this hypothesis in mind that I record something which happened this morning.

I entered the Second North-Eastern Hall and, as had happened in the Ninth Vestibule, I found it full of small birds of different sorts. I called a cheerful Good morning! to them.

Immediately twenty or so flew in a great rush to the Northern Wall and alighted on the High Statues. Then they flew in a swoop to the Western Wall.

I recalled that on the previous occasion this behaviour had been the preface to a message.

'I am paying attention!' I called to them. 'What is it that you wish to say to me?'

I watched very carefully what they did next.

The birds separated into two groups. One group flew to the Statue of an Angel blowing a Trumpet; the other group flew to the Statue of a Ship that travels on little Waves.

'An angel with a trumpet and a ship,' I said. 'Very well.'

The first group flew to a Statue of a Man reading from a large Book; the second group flew to a Statue of a Woman displaying a large Dish or Shield; upon the Shield is a representation of Clouds.

'A book and clouds,' I said. 'Yes.'

Finally the first group flew to the Statue of a little Child bowing its Head to gaze at a Flower, which it holds in its Hand; the Child's Head is covered with such exuberant Curls they are themselves like the petals of a flower; the second group of birds flew to a Statue of a Sack of Grain being devoured by a Horde of Mice.

'A child and mice,' I said. 'Very good. I see.'

The birds dispersed to different places in the Hall.

'Thank you!' I called to them. 'Thank you!'

Supposing my hypothesis to be correct, this is certainly the most elaborate communication that the birds have offered me. What is the meaning?

An angel with a trumpet and a ship. An angel with a trumpet suggests a message. A joyful message? Perhaps. But an angel might also bring a stern or solemn message. Therefore the character of the message, whether good or bad, remains uncertain. The ship suggests travelling long distances. *A message coming from afar.*

A book and clouds. A book contains Writing. Clouds hide what is there. *Writing that is somehow obscure.*

A child and mice. The child represents the quality of Innocence. The mice are devouring the grain. Little by little it is diminished. *Innocence that is worn down or eroded.*

So this, as far as I can tell, is what the birds told me. *A message from afar. Obscure Writing. Innocence eroded.*

Interesting.

I will allow some time to elapse – say a few months – and then I will examine this communication again to see if the intervening events can shed any light upon it (and vice versa).

Addy Domarus
ENTRY FOR THE FIFTEENTH DAY OF THE SIXTH MONTH IN THE
YEAR THE ALBATROSS CAME TO THE SOUTH-WESTERN HALLS

This morning in the Second South-Western Hall the Other said, 'I'm going to be working on the ritual today so you may not want to stick around.'

The Ritual is a piece of ceremonial magic by which the Other intends to free the Great and Secret Knowledge from whatever holds it captive in the World and to transfer it to ourselves. So far, we have performed it four times, each time in a slightly different version.

'I've made some changes,' he continued, 'and I want to hear how they sound, *in situ* as it were.'

'I will help you,' I said, eagerly.

'Fine,' he said. 'Just as long as you don't get too chatty. I need focus. Clarity.'

'Absolutely,' I said.

Today the Other was wearing a suit of mid-grey with a white shirt and black shoes. He laid his shining device upon the Empty Plinth. 'This is a summoning, and in summonings, the seer ought to face east,' he said. 'Which way's east?'

I pointed.

'Right,' he said.

'Where shall I stand?'

'Wherever you like. It doesn't matter.'

I took up a position two metres South of the place where he was standing and decided that I would face North – that is, towards him. I have no real insight or knowledge concerning rituals, but this seemed to me an appropriate position for an acolyte, subservient yet connected to the Interpreter of Mysteries.

'What shall I do?' I asked.

'Nothing. Just keep quiet like I told you.'

'I will concentrate on lending you the strength of my Spirit,' I said.

'Fine. Good. You do that.' He returned briefly to his shining device to check something. 'OK,' he said. 'This first part of the ritual is where I've made most changes. Up to now I've been simply invoking the knowledge and asking it to come to me and bestow itself upon me. That doesn't seem to have got me anywhere so instead I'm going to summon the spirit of Addy Domarus.'

'Who or what is Addy Domarus?' I asked.

'A king. Long dead. Someone who possessed the knowledge. Or some of it at any rate. I've had success calling on him for aid in other rituals, notably for … ' He stopped abruptly and for a brief moment looked confused. 'I've had success calling on him in the past,' he finished.

The Other assumed the noble posture of an Interpreter of Mysteries. He straightened his back, pulled back his shoulders and lifted up his head. He put me in mind of the Statue of a Hierophant in the Nineteenth Southern Hall.

Suddenly the significance of what he had said struck me.

'Oh!' I exclaimed. 'You have never said before that you knew one of the names of the Dead! Do you know which one he is? Please tell me if you do! I would very much like to call him by his name when I take him offerings of food and drink!'

The Other stopped what he was doing and frowned. 'What?' he said.

'The Dead,' I went on, eagerly. 'If you do indeed know one of their names, then please tell me to which of them it belongs.'

'Sorry? You've lost me. Which of the what was what?'

'You said that in times gone by one or more of the Dead possessed the Knowledge. Then they lost it. So I wanted to know which of them it was. The Biscuit-Box Man? The Concealed Person? Or was it one of the People of the Alcove?'

The Other gazed at me blankly. 'Biscuit box … What are you talking about? Oh, wait. Is this something to do with those bones you found? No. No-no-no-no-no. Those aren't … That's not … Oh, for God's sake! Didn't I just say that I need to focus? Didn't I just say that? Can we not do this now? I'm trying to get this ritual sorted.'

Immediately I felt ashamed. I was impeding the Other's important work. 'Yes, of course,' I said.

'I don't have time to answer irrelevant questions,' he snapped.

'Sorry.'

'If you could just be quiet, that would be wonderful.'

'I will,' I said. 'I promise.'

'Fine. Good. OK. Where was I?' said the Other. He took a deep breath and stood very erect again, rearing up his head. He raised his arms and in sonorous tones he called on Addy Domarus several times and in several different ways to *Come! Come!*

In the ensuing silence he gradually let his arms fall to his sides, and relaxed. 'OK,' he said. 'For the real thing I'll maybe have a brazier. Some incense burning. We'll see. Then after the invocation comes the enumeration. I name the powers I seek: the vanquishing of Death, the penetration of lesser minds, invisibility etc., etc. It's important to visualise each power and so, as I name them, I imagine myself living forever, reading someone else's thoughts, becoming invisible and so on.'

I raised my hand politely. (I did not want to be accused of asking irrelevant questions again.)

'Yes?' he said, sharply.

'Shall I do that too?'

'Yes. If you like.'

In the same sonorous voice the Other recited the list of powers that the Knowledge bestows, and when he intoned, *I name the power of flight!*, I pictured Myself transformed into an osprey, flying with the other ospreys over the Surging Tides. (Of all the powers that the Other talks about, this is my favourite. To be perfectly honest, I am largely indifferent to the rest.

What use would invisibility be to me? Most days there is no one here to see me except the birds. Nor do I have any desire to live forever. The House ordains a certain span for birds and another for men. With this I am content.)

The Other reached the end of his list. I could see that he was thinking about the parts of the ritual he had just performed and that he was not satisfied with them. There was a scowl on his face, and he stared off into the distance. 'I feel like I should be addressing all this to some sort of – some kind of energy, something vital and alive. It is power that I seek and therefore I should be speaking these words to something that is already powerful. Does that make sense?'

'Yes,' I said.

'But there isn't anything powerful. There isn't even anything alive. Just endless dreary rooms all the same, full of decaying figures covered with bird shit.' He fell into an unhappy silence.

I have known for many years that the Other does not revere the House in the same way I do, but it still shocks me when he talks like this. How can a man as intelligent as him say there is nothing alive in the House? The Lower Halls are full of sea creatures and vegetation, many of them very beautiful and very strange. The Tides themselves are full of movement and power so that, while they may not exactly be alive, neither are they not-alive. In the Middle Halls are birds and men. The droppings (of which he complains) are signs of Life! Nor is he correct to say that the Halls are all the same. They vary a great deal in the style of their Columns, Pilasters, Niches, Apses, Pediments etc., as well as in the number of their Doors and Windows. Every Hall has its Statues and all the Statues are unique, or if there are any repetitions they must occur at vast distances as I have yet to see one.

There was, however, no point in saying any of this. I knew that it would only irritate him further.

'What about a Star?' I said. 'If we perform the Ritual at night, you can address the Invocation to a Star. A Star is a source of power and energy.'

A moment's silence, then: 'That's true,' he said. He sounded surprised. 'A star. That's actually not a bad idea.' He thought some more. 'A fixed star would be better than a wandering one. And it would need to be bright – appreciably brighter than the surrounding stars. What would be best would be to find somewhere in the labyrinth, some point or place that's unique – and to perform the ritual there, facing the brightest star!' For a moment he was full of excitement. Then he sighed and all the energy seemed to drain out of him again. 'But that's not very likely, is it?' Then he said again that every Hall was exactly like every other Hall, except that he called them 'rooms' and used an epithet meant to denigrate them.

I felt a surge of anger and for a moment I thought I would not tell him what I knew. But then I thought that it was unkind to punish him for something he cannot help. It is not his fault that he does not see things the way I do.

'Actually,' I said, 'there is one Hall different from the others.'

'Oh?' he said. 'You never said anything about it. In what way is it different?'

'It has only one Doorway and no Windows. I only saw it once. It has a strange atmosphere that is difficult to describe precisely. It is majestic, mysterious and at the same time, full of Presence.'

'You mean like a temple?' he said.

'Yes. Like a temple.'

'Why didn't you tell me about this before?' he demanded, his anger and irritation rising again.

'Well, it is some distance from here. I thought that you were unlikely to ... '

But he was not interested in my explanation. 'I need to see this place. Can you take me? How far is it?'

'It is the One-Hundred-and-Ninety-Second Western Hall and it is 20 kilometres from the First Vestibule,' I said. 'It takes 3.76 hours to reach it, not including rest periods.'

'Oh,' he said.

I knew that I could scarcely have said anything more discouraging to him (though that was not my intention). He has no desire to explore the World. I do not believe that he has ever travelled more than the length of four or five Halls from the First Vestibule.

He said, 'What I need to know is what stars can be seen from the door of this room. Have you any idea?'

I thought. Had the One-Hundred-and-Ninety-Second Western Hall been oriented along an East/West axis? Or was it a South-East/North-West axis? I shook my head. 'I do not know. I cannot remember.'

'Well, can't you go back and find out?' he demanded.

'Go to the One-Hundred-and-Ninety-Second Western Hall?'

'Yes.'

I hesitated.

'What's the problem?' he asked.

'The Path to the One-Hundred-and-Ninety-Second Western Hall lies through the Seventy-Eighth Vestibule, a Region subject to frequent flooding. Just now it will be dry, but the Tides bring up Debris from the Lower Halls and scatter it throughout the surrounding Halls. Some of the Debris has jagged edges, which can cut a person's feet. It is not good to have bleeding feet. There is a danger of infection. A person must pick their way carefully through the Broken Marble. It is possible, but laborious. It will take time.'

'OK,' said the Other. 'So there's debris. But I'm still not really understanding what the problem is. You must have passed through this place where the debris is before and you didn't come to any harm then. What's changed?'

A blush rose to my face. I fixed my eyes on the Pavement. The Other was so neat, so elegant in his suit and his shining shoes. I, on the other hand, was not neat. My clothes were ragged and faded, rotten with the Sea Water I fished in. I hated drawing his attention to this contrast between us, but nevertheless he had asked me and so I must answer. I said, 'What changed was that I used to have shoes. Now I have none.'

The Other gazed in astonishment at my naked brown feet. 'When did this happen?'

'About a year ago. My shoes fell apart.'

He burst out laughing. 'Why didn't you say something?'

'I did not want to trouble you. I thought I could make some shoes out of fish leather. But I have not found the time to do it. I have only myself to blame.'

'Honestly, Piranesi,' said the Other. 'What an idiot you are! If that's all that's preventing you going to the ... the ... whatever you call this room ... '

'The One-Hundred-and-Ninety-Second Western Hall,' I interjected.

'Yes. Whatever. If that's all it is, I'll get you the shoes tomorrow.'

'Oh! That would be ... ' I began, but the Other put up his hand.

'No need to thank me. Just get me the information I need. That's all I ask.'

'Oh, I will!' I promised. 'Once I have shoes there will be no problem. I will reach the One-Hundred-and-Ninety-Second Western Hall in three-and-a-half hours. Four at the most.'

Shoes

ENTRY FOR THE SIXTEENTH DAY OF THE SIXTH MONTH IN THE YEAR THE ALBATROSS CAME TO THE SOUTH-WESTERN HALLS

On the way to the Third South-Western Hall this morning I passed through the Second South-Western Hall. On top of the Empty Plinth where the Other leans was a small cardboard box. It was a deep grey colour. On the lid was a picture of an octopus in a paler shade of grey and some orange writing. The writing said: AQUARIUM.

I opened it. At first sight it appeared to contain nothing except thin white paper, but when I lifted the paper I found a pair of shoes. They were made of canvas of a blue-green colour that reminded me of the Tides of the Southern Halls. The rubber soles were thick and white and they had white laces. I removed them from the box and put them on. They fitted perfectly. I tried walking about in them. My feet felt beautifully cushioned and bouncible.

All day long I have been running and dancing for the sheer pleasure of feeling my feet in their new shoes.

'Look!' I said to the crows in the First Northern Hall when they flew down from the High Statues to see what I was doing, 'I have new shoes!'

But the crows only cawed and flew back to their perches.

A list of things the Other has given me
ENTRY FOR THE SEVENTEENTH DAY OF THE SIXTH MONTH IN THE YEAR THE ALBATROSS CAME TO THE SOUTH-WESTERN HALLS

I have made a list of all the things that the Other has given me, so that I will remember to be grateful and thank the House for sending me such an excellent friend!

In the Year I named the Constellations, the Other gave me:

- a sleeping bag
- a pillow
- 2 blankets
- 2 fishing nets made of a synthetic polymer
- 4 large sheets of heavy-gauge plastic
- a torch. I have never used this and cannot now remember where I put it.
- 6 boxes of matches
- 2 bottles of multivitamins

In the Year I counted and named the Dead, he gave me:

- a cheese and ham sandwich

In the Year that the Ceilings in the Twentieth and Twenty-First North-Eastern Halls collapsed, he gave me:

- 6 plastic bowls. I use them to catch Fresh Water as it flows through Cracks in the Ceilings and down the Faces of the Statues. One of the bowls is blue, two are red and three are cloud coloured. The cloud-coloured ones are troublesome. They are almost exactly the same whitey-grey colour as the Statues. Whenever I put them somewhere to catch Water they immediately fade into their surroundings and I lose sight of them. One disappeared last year and I have yet to find it.
- 4 pairs of socks. For two Winters my feet have been warm and cosy, but now the socks are all in holes. Unfortunately, it has not occurred to the Other to give me new ones.
- a fishing rod and line
- an orange
- a slice of Christmas cake
- 8 bottles of multivitamins
- 4 boxes of matches

In the Year I travelled to the Nine-Hundred-and-Sixtieth Western Hall, he gave me:

- a new battery for my watch
- 10 new notebooks
- various assorted items of stationery, including 12 large sheets of paper to make Star Maps, envelopes, pencils, a ruler and some rubbers

- 47 pens
- more multivitamins and matches

This year (the Year the Albatross came to the South-Western Halls), he has given me so far:

- 3 more plastic bowls. These are the best ones, being brightly coloured and therefore easy to see. One is orange and two are different shades of green.
- 4 boxes of matches
- 3 bottles of vitamins
- a pair of new shoes!

I owe so much to the Other's generosity. Without him I would not sleep snug and warm in my sleeping bag in Winter. I would not have notebooks in which to record my thoughts.

That being said, it occurs to me to wonder why it is that the House gives a greater variety of objects to the Other than to me, providing him with sleeping bags, shoes, plastic bowls, cheese sandwiches, notebooks, slices of Christmas cake etc., etc., whereas me it mostly gives fish. I think perhaps it is because the Other is not as skilled in taking care of himself as I am. He does not know how to fish. He never (as far as I know) gathers seaweed, dries it and stores it to make fires or a tasty snack; he does not cure fish skins and make leather out of them (which is useful for many things). If the House did not provide all these things for him, it is quite possible that he would die. Or else (which is more likely) I would have to devote a great deal of my time to caring for him.

None of the Dead claim the name Addy Domarus

It has been some weeks since I visited the Dead and so today I did so. It is no small undertaking to visit them all in the space of one day since they lie several kilometres distant from each other. I brought each one an offering of water and food, and water lilies that I had gathered in the Drowned Halls.

At each of the Niches and Plinths I whispered the name *Addy Domarus*. I hoped that one of them – the one to whom the name belongs – would somehow communicate his acceptance of it. But that did not happen. Rather, as I knelt at each Niche or Plinth, I felt a faint sense of repudiation, as if the name were being pushed away.

A journey

I spent today working at my usual tasks: fishing, gathering seaweed, working on my Catalogue of Statues. In the late afternoon I gathered some supplies and set out to walk to the One-Hundred-and-Ninety-Second Western Hall.

On the way the House showed me many wonders.

In the Forty-Fifth Vestibule I saw a Staircase that had become one vast bed of mussels. One of the Statues that lined the Wall of the Staircase was all but engulfed in a blue-black carapace of mussels with only half a staring Face and one white, out-flung Arm left free. I made a sketch of it in my Journal.

In the Fifty-Second Western Hall I came upon a Wall ablaze with so much golden Light that the Statues appeared to be dissolving into it. From there I passed into a little Antechamber with few Windows, where it was cool and shadowy. I saw the Statue of a Woman holding out a wide, flat Dish so that a Bear Cub could drink from it.

As I approached the Seventy-Eighth Vestibule, the Pavements were strewn with Rubble. At first, I saw only a scattering here and there, but by the time I drew close to the Vestibule I was walking over an uneven and treacherous Floor of Jagged Stones. In the Vestibule itself a thin sheet of Water still ran beneath the Rubble. Broken Statues were heaped in the Corners.

I walked on. In the Eighty-Eighth Western Hall the Pavement was free from Debris, but I found another problem. A colony of herring gulls had built their nests in this Hall and my intrusion among them was met with fury. They squawked indignantly and flew at me, beating their wings and attempting to peck at me with their beaks. I waved my arms and shouted to ward them off.

I reached the One-Hundred-and-Ninety-Second Western Hall. I stood at the Single Door and peered inside. The surrounding Halls were full of a soft blue Twilight but this particular Hall – which, as I have already said, has no Windows – was dark, its Statues invisible. A faint draught – like a cold breath – emanated from it.

I am not accustomed to Absolute Darkness. There are very few Dark Places in the House; perhaps here and there you will find the Shadowy Corner of an Antechamber or an Angle of the Derelict Halls where the Light is blocked by Debris; but generally, the House is not dark. Even at night the Stars blaze down through the Windows.

I had imagined that all I would need to do to answer the Other's question – What Stars can be seen from the door of the Hall? – was to ascertain the exact orientation of the Hall and then consult my Star Maps. But now that I was actually at the Door, I realised that this plan was wildly optimistic. The Door was approximately four metres wide and eleven metres high, which is huge for a Door but minuscule when compared to the vastness of the Sky. I would not be able to tell which Stars would be framed in the Doorway unless I spent the night in the Hall and saw for Myself.

I did not find this prospect appealing.

I remembered how I climbed a Staircase to the Upper Hall above the Nineteenth Eastern Hall and found it filled with Cloud. I remembered how that Hall was full of gigantic Figures in the throes of violent action, how every Face was distorted by screams of rage or anguish.

Suppose (I thought) this happened again? Suppose I went into the Darkness of the One-Hundred-and-Ninety-Second Western Hall and I lay down to sleep, only to wake and find Myself surrounded by horrors?

I became angry at Myself, disgusted at my own timidity. This was no way to think! Had I walked for four hours to reach this Hall only to be too afraid to go in? How ridiculous! I told Myself that the fear I had experienced in that Upper Hall was highly unlikely to be repeated anywhere else. I had, after all, entered the One-Hundred-and-Ninety-Second Western Hall before. If the Statues had been particularly violent or frightening, I would surely have remembered. Besides, I had an obligation to the Other. He needed to know what Stars were visible from the Door.

But still the Darkness unnerved me. I put off entering it for a while. I sat down outside and ate and drank and wrote this entry in my Journal.

The One-Hundred-and-Ninety-Second Western Hall
ENTRY FOR THE TWENTIETH DAY OF THE SIXTH MONTH IN THE YEAR THE ALBATROSS CAME TO THE SOUTH-WESTERN HALLS

Having completed the previous entry in my Journal I entered the One-Hundred-and-Ninety-Second Western Hall. Dark and Cold enveloped me. A little way in (I estimate about twenty metres) I turned to face the Single Door that aligned perfectly with a Window in the Corridor outside. I sat down and wrapped Myself in my blanket.

At first I was acutely conscious of the Darkness at my back and the stares of the Unknown Statues. It was very quiet. The Hall where I usually sleep – the Third Northern Hall – is full of birds and at night I hear the little sounds as they shift and flutter on their perches; but as far as I could tell there were no birds in the One-Hundred-and-Ninety-Second Western Hall. They apparently found it as unsettling as I did.

I made Myself focus on the one thing familiar to me: the sound of the Sea in the Lower Halls, the Water lapping the

Walls in a thousand, thousand Chambers. It is a sound that accompanies me all my days. I fall asleep to it every night, just as a child might fall asleep, safe on its mother's breast, listening to her heartbeat. And indeed, this is what must have happened now, because the next thing I knew was that I was waking suddenly out of sleep.

A Full Moon stood in the centre of the Single Doorway, flooding the Hall with Light. The Statues on the Walls were all posed as if they had just turned to face the Doorway, their marble Eyes fixed on the Moon. They were different from the Statues in other Halls; they were not isolated individuals, but the representation of a Crowd. Here were two with their Arms about each other; here one had his Hand on the Shoulder of one in front, the better to pull himself forward to see the Moon; here a Child held on to its Father's Hand. There was even a Dog that — having no interest in the Moon — stood on its Hind Legs, its Front Paws on its Master's Chest, pleading for attention. The Rear Wall was a mass of Statues — not neatly arranged in Tiers, but a jumbled, chaotic Crowd. Foremost among them was a Young Man, who stood bathed in the Moonlight, elation in his Face, a Banner in his Hand.

I almost forgot to breathe. For a moment I had an inkling of what it might be like if instead of two people in the World there were thousands.

The Eighty-Eighth Western Hall
SECOND ENTRY FOR THE TWENTIETH DAY OF THE SIXTH MONTH IN THE YEAR THE ALBATROSS CAME TO THE SOUTH-WESTERN HALLS

The Full Moon declined westwards, the Light in the Hall diminished and the Constellations grew brighter in the Window opposite the Doorway. I made notes of what Constellations and Stars I saw. At Dawn I slept for a few hours and then I began the journey home.

As I walked, I was thinking about the Great and Secret Knowledge, which the Other says will grant us strange new powers. And I realised something. I realised that I no longer believed in it. Or perhaps that is not quite accurate. I thought it was possible that the Knowledge existed. Equally I thought that it was possible it did not. Either way it no longer mattered to me. I did not intend to waste my time looking for it any more.

This realisation – the realisation of the Insignificance of the Knowledge – came to me in the form of a Revelation. What I mean by this is that I knew it to be true before I understood why or what steps had led me there. When I tried to retrace those steps my mind kept returning to the image of the One-Hundred-and-Ninety-Second Western Hall in the Moonlight, to its Beauty, to its deep sense of Calm, to the reverent looks on the Faces of the Statues as they turned (or seemed to turn) towards the Moon. I realised that the search for the Knowledge has encouraged us to think of the House as if it were a sort of riddle to be unravelled, a text to be interpreted, and that if ever we discover the Knowledge, then it will be as if the Value has been wrested from the House and all that remains will be mere scenery.

The sight of the One-Hundred-and-Ninety-Second Western Hall in the Moonlight made me see how ridiculous that is. The

House is valuable because it is the House. It is enough in and of Itself. It is not the means to an end.

This thought led on to another. I realised that the Other's description of the powers that the Knowledge will grant has always made me uneasy. For example: he says that we will have the power to control lesser minds. Well, to begin with there are no lesser minds; there are only him and me and we both have keen and lively intellects. But, supposing for a moment that a lesser mind existed, why would I want to control it?

Abandoning the search for the Knowledge would free us to pursue a new sort of science. We could follow any path that the data suggested to us. The thought of all this made me excited and happy. I was eager to return to the Other and explain it to him.

I was walking through the Halls, thinking of these things, when I heard the raucous cries of birds and I remembered that the Eighty-Eighth Western Hall was full of herring gulls. I wondered whether or not to take a different Path, but, estimating that any diversion would add seven or eight Halls (1.7 kilometres) to my journey, I decided against it.

I had got halfway across the Hall when I noticed a scattering of white shapes lying on the Pavement. I picked them up. They were pieces of torn paper with writing on them. They were crumpled and so I smoothed them out and tried putting them together. Two – no, three – of the scraps fitted perfectly, forming part of a small sheet of paper with one jagged side. It appeared to be a page torn from a notebook.

I could see that, even when reconstructed, the page would be difficult to decipher. The writing was atrocious – like a tangle of seaweed. After some minutes of peering at it I thought I could make out the word 'minotaur'. A line or two above I thought I saw the word 'slave' and a line or two below the phrase 'kill him'. The rest was completely impenetrable. But the reference to a 'minotaur' intrigued me. The First Vestibule contains eight massive Statues of Minotaurs, each one different from the others. Perhaps the person who had written this had visited my own Halls?

I wondered whose writing it could be. Not the Other's. Aside from the fact that I was sure he had never ventured as far as the Eighty-Eighth Western Hall, I knew his writing to be neat and precise. One of the Dead then. The Fish-Leather Man? The Biscuit-Box Man? The Concealed Person? Potentially this was a discovery of great historical importance.

Now that I knew what I was looking for I could see more white shapes lying on the Pavement. I set about gathering them up. Beginning in the South-Western Corner I worked my way systematically over the Pavement of the entire Hall, covering every part of it. At first the herring gulls made raucous objection to my doing this, but when they saw that I did not come near their eggs or young, they lost interest. I found forty-seven pieces of paper, but when I knelt and tried to fit them all together it became clear that many more were still missing.

I looked around. Herring gull nests were perched on the Shoulders of Statues and crammed onto Plinths; there was one tucked between the Legs of the Statue of an Elephant and another balanced in the Crown of an Elderly King. Peeking out of the nest in the Crown I could see two white fragments. Cautiously I approached and climbed up a neighbouring Statue to examine it. Immediately two gulls attacked me, screaming their indignation and dashing at me with wings and beaks. But I was equally determined. With one arm I hauled Myself up the Statue and with the other I beat back the birds.

The nest was a ramshackle, untidy thing built of dry seaweed and fishbones; woven into its structure were five or six scraps of paper with writing on them. I dismounted and retreated to the middle of the Hall away from the Walls, the nests and the attacking gulls.

I considered what I ought to do. There was no possibility of retrieving the missing pieces now. The herring gulls would never permit me to dismantle their nests – nor did I want to. No, I must wait until late summer – or, even better, early autumn – when the gulls had abandoned the nests and the young were grown. Then I could come back and get all the missing pieces.

I placed the forty-seven pieces carefully in my pack and continued my journey home.

The Other explains that he has said all this before
ENTRY FOR THE TWENTY-SECOND DAY OF THE SIXTH MONTH IN THE YEAR THE ALBATROSS CAME TO THE SOUTH-WESTERN HALLS

This morning I took my Star Maps to the Second South-Western Hall.

I found the Other leaning back against the Empty Plinth, his ankles crossed and his elbows resting on the Plinth. He looked relaxed. He wore an immaculate suit of a dark navy colour and a brilliant white shirt. He gave me a friendly smile. 'How're the shoes?' he asked.

'Excellent!' I said. 'Brilliant! Thank you! But what I value even more than the shoes themselves is the proof they give of our friendship! I consider the possession of such a friend as you to be one of the greatest happinesses of my Life!'

'I do my best,' said the Other. 'So tell me. How have you been getting on? Now that you've got the shoes.'

'I have already visited the One-Hundred-and-Ninety-Second Western Hall!'

'OK. And did you see what stars there were? Did you make notes?'

'I did make notes,' I said. 'But I have not brought them with me since I remember everything I have to tell you.'

Then I told him what I had seen in the One-Hundred-and-Ninety-Second Western Hall. 'The Statues are its most remarkable feature. I mean other than the Single Door and the No-Windows. The Moonlight picked out one Statue in particular – the image of a Young Man. He seemed to me to represent the Virtues of—'

'Don't bother with all that. You know I'm not interested in statues. Tell me about the stars,' said the Other. 'What could you see?'

'I will show you.' I opened one of my Star Maps and placed it on the top of the Empty Plinth. He came and stood by me. 'I saw the Rose, the Good Mother and the Lamp-post. Towards morning these were followed by the Shoemaker and the Iron Snake.' (These were some of the names I had given the Constellations.)

The Other examined the Map carefully. Then he picked up his shining device and made some notes.

'Are any of these stars particularly bright?' he asked.

'Yes. This Star here. It forms part of the Good Mother. It is the tip of her extended arm, so to speak. It is one of the brightest Stars in the Sky.'

'Perfect,' said the Other. 'The brightest star to symbolise the greatest knowledge. Well, while you've been doing all that I've come to a decision. I've decided that I will go to this room and perform the ritual there. Obviously it's much further into the labyrinth than I've ever been before, so there are risks … ' He paused for a moment and looked very determined, as if steeling himself to something. ' … but balancing the risks against the rewards – well, the rewards are potentially immense. This information you've brought me is invaluable and what I need you to do now is to go back there and establish what constellations can be seen at different times of year.'

Now was the time for me to explain my Revelation concerning the Great and Secret Knowledge.

'As to that,' I said, 'I too have something to say. Something has been revealed to me that I must now share with you, something that has far-reaching implications for all our future research. We must cease our search for the Knowledge! When we began, we believed that it was a worthy endeavour, deserving all our attention, but it turns out that it is not. We should abandon it straightaway and, in its place, establish a new programme of scientific research!'

The Other was not paying attention. He was making notes on his shining device. 'Mmm? What?' he said.

'I am speaking of our search for the Knowledge,' I said, 'and of how the House has revealed to me that we should abandon it.'

The Other stopped tapping. He took a moment to process what I had just said. Then he put the device down on the Empty Plinth, covered his face with his hands, made a sort of groaning noise and massaged his eyes. 'Oh, God! Not this again,' he said.

He uncovered his eyes. He turned away and stared off into the distance. 'Don't say anything,' he said (though I had not uttered another word). 'I need to think.'

There was a long silence at the end of which he seemed to come to a decision. 'Sit down,' he said.

We sat down together on the Pavement of the Hall. I sat cross-legged and he sat with his knees bent, his back against the Empty Plinth.

There was a sort of glowering darkness in his face. He seemed to be finding it difficult to look at me. By these signs I knew that he was angry but struggling not to show it.

He coughed. 'OK,' he said in a controlled voice. 'There are three reasons – three – why you shouldn't stop looking for the knowledge. I'm going to go through all of them now and at the end, I think you'll see I'm right. I just need you to listen to me. You can do that, can't you?'

'Of course,' I said. 'Tell me the three reasons.'

'OK, the first reason is this. It may seem to you that what I'm doing is rather selfish – trying to get the knowledge for myself. But the reality is quite different. This search that you and I are embarked on, it's a truly great project. Momentous. One of the most important in humanity's history. The knowledge we seek isn't something new. It's old. Really old. Once upon a time people possessed it and they used it to do great things, miraculous things. They should have held on to it. They should have respected it. But they didn't. They abandoned it for the sake of something they called progress. And it's up to us to get it back. We're not doing this for ourselves; we're doing it for humanity. To get back something humanity has foolishly lost.'

'I see,' I said. (This did indeed put things in a slightly different light.)

'And personally,' continued the Other, 'I think that this search is so important, so absolutely vital that I have to keep going. No matter what. I don't have any choice. If your decision is to stop looking – well, in that case I suppose we'd no longer be colleagues. Our meetings on Tuesdays and Fridays – we'd no longer have them. Because what would be the point? I'd be pursuing my researches and you'd be off' – he gestured vaguely –'doing whatever it is that you do. This isn't what I want of course, let me be very clear about that, but it is the way things would have to be. So that's the second reason.'

'Oh!' I said. It had never occurred to me that he and I would cease to be colleagues. 'But working with you is one of the great pleasures of my life!'

'I know,' said the Other. 'And of course, I feel the same way.' He paused. 'Now I need to tell you the third reason. But before I do that, I need you to hear something else.' He gazed intently and searchingly into my face. 'This is the most vital thing I have to say. Piranesi, this isn't the first time you've told me that you want to stop the search for the knowledge. This isn't the first time I've explained why that's not the right course of action. Everything we've just said? *We've said it all before.*'

'I ... What?' I said. I blinked at him in astonishment. 'What? ... No. No. That is not correct.'

'Yes, I'm afraid it is. You see, the labyrinth plays tricks on the mind. It makes people forget things. If you're not careful it can unpick your entire personality.'

I sat dumbfounded. 'How many times have we said it?' I said at last.

He thought for a moment. 'This is the third time. There's a pattern. The idea of stopping the search for the knowledge seems to occur to you roughly once every eighteen months.' He glanced at my face. 'I know. I know,' he said, sympathetic-ally. 'It's hard to take in.'

'But I do not understand,' I protested. 'I have an excellent memory. I remember every Hall I have ever visited. There are seven thousand, six hundred and seventy-eight of them.'

'You never forget anything about the labyrinth. That is why your contribution to my work is so valuable. But you do forget other things. And, of course, you lose time.'

'What?' I said, startled.

'Time. You're always losing it.'

'What do you mean?'

'You know. You get days and dates wrong.'

'I do not,' I said, indignant.

'Yes, you do. It's a bit of a pain, to be honest. My schedule's always so packed. I come to meet you and you're nowhere to be seen because you've lost a day again. I've had to put you right numerous times when your perception of time has got out of sync.'

'Out of sync with what?'

'With me. With everyone else.'

I was astonished. I did not believe him. But neither did I disbelieve him. I did not know what to think. But in all my uncertainty one thing was clear, one thing remained that I could absolutely rely on: the Other was honest, noble and industrious. He would not lie. 'But why do *you* not forget?' I asked.

The Other hesitated for a moment. 'I take precautions,' he said carefully.

'Could I not take them too?'

'No. No. That wouldn't work. Sorry. I can't go into the whys and wherefores. It's complicated. I'll explain it to you one day.'

This was not very satisfactory but just then I did not have the energy or mental capacity to pursue it. I was too busy thinking about what I might have forgotten.

'From my point of view this is very worrying,' I said. 'Suppose I forget something important, like the Times and Patterns of the Tides? I might drown.'

'No, no, no,' said the Other, soothingly. 'There's no need to worry about that. You never forget anything like that. I wouldn't let you go wandering about if I thought you were in the slightest danger. We've known each other for years now and in that time your knowledge of the labyrinth has grown exponentially. It's extraordinary, really. And as for the rest, anything important you forget, I can remind you. But the fact that you forget while I remember – that's why it's so vital that I set our objectives. Me. Not you. That's the third reason we should stick to our search for the knowledge. Do you see?'

'Yes. Yes. At least … ' I was silent a moment. 'I need time to think,' I said.

'Of course. Of course,' said the Other. He patted me consolingly on the shoulder. 'We'll discuss it again on Tuesday.'

He rose to his feet and went over to the Empty Plinth and examined the little shining device lying there. 'In any case,' he said, 'I need to get going. I've been here almost fifty-five minutes.' Without another word he turned and set off in the direction of the First Vestibule.

The World does not bear out the Other's claim that there are gaps in my memory

ENTRY FOR THE TWENTY-THIRD DAY OF THE SIXTH MONTH IN THE YEAR THE ALBATROSS CAME TO THE SOUTH-WESTERN HALLS

The World (so far as I can tell) does not bear out the Other's claim that there are gaps in my memory.

While he was explaining it to me – and for some time afterwards – I did not know what to think. At several points I experienced a feeling akin to panic. Could it really be the case that I had forgotten whole conversations?

But as the day went on, I could find no evidence of memory loss to support the Other's claim. I busied Myself with my ordinary, everyday tasks. I mended one of my fishing nets and worked on my Catalogue of Statues. In the early evening I went to the Eighth Vestibule to fish in the Waters of the Lower Staircase. The Beams of the Declining Sun shone through the Windows of the Lower Halls, striking the Surface of the Waves and making ripples of golden Light flow across the Ceiling of the Staircase and over the Faces of the Statues. When night fell, I listened to the Songs that the Moon and Stars were singing and I sang with them.

The World feels Complete and Whole, and I, its Child, fit into it seamlessly. Nowhere is there any disjuncture where I ought to remember something but do not, where I ought to understand something but do not. The only part of my existence in which I experience any sense of fragmentation is in that last strange conversation with the Other. And so I have to ask Myself: whose memory is at fault? Mine or his? Might he in fact be remembering conversations that never happened?

Two memories. Two bright minds which remember past events differently. It is an awkward situation. There exists no third person to say which of us is correct. (If only the Sixteenth Person were here!)

As for the Other's claim that I lose time and muddle days, I do not see how this can possibly be true. I invented the calendar I use, so how could it get 'out of sync' as he put it? There is nothing for it to get out of sync with.

I wonder now if this is why he asked me that strange question three and a half weeks ago? I mean the question with a strange word in it. Turning back the pages of my Journal I see that the strange word was 'Batter-Sea'.

And then, in an instant, the solution presents itself! All I have to do is read through my Journals and discover if there are any discrepancies, any events recorded there that I no longer recall. Yes! This will certainly decide the matter. In fact, the only drawback with this idea is that it will take a substantial amount of time – my writings being lengthy – which I cannot just now spare from other projects.

I am resolved to read through my Journals at some point in the coming months and in the meantime shall proceed on the assumption that it is the Other's memory, and not mine, which is incorrect.

I write a letter
ENTRY FOR THE TWENTY-FOURTH DAY OF THE SIXTH MONTH IN THE YEAR THE ALBATROSS CAME TO THE SOUTH-WESTERN HALLS

The following is a transcript of the letter that I inscribed in chalk on the Pavement of the Second South-Western Hall.

DEAR OTHER

ALTHOUGH I CANNOT ANY LONGER REGARD THE SEARCH FOR THE GREAT AND SECRET KNOWLEDGE AS A LEGITIMATE SCIENTIFIC ENDEAVOUR, I HAVE DETERMINED THAT THE CORRECT COURSE OF ACTION IS TO CONTINUE TO HELP YOU AND GATHER ANY DATA YOU REQUIRE. IT IS NOT RIGHT THAT YOUR SCIENTIFIC WORK SHOULD SUFFER SIMPLY BECAUSE I HAVE LOST CONFIDENCE IN THE HYPOTHESIS. I HOPE THAT THIS IS ACCEPTABLE TO YOU.

YOUR FRIEND

The Other warns me about 16

This morning I went to the Second South-Western Hall to meet the Other. I confess that I was a little anxious about how the meeting would go. Sometimes when I am anxious, I talk a lot, and so I immediately launched on a long speech, elaborating quite unnecessarily on the letter I had chalked on the Pavement.

It did not matter. Halfway through I realised that the Other was not listening. His head was bent in thought and he was absent-mindedly turning over some small metallic objects in the pocket of his jacket. Today he wore a suit of a dark charcoal colour and a black shirt.

'You haven't seen anyone else in the labyrinth, have you?' he said suddenly.

'Someone else?' I said.

'Yes.'

'Someone new?' I said.

'Yes,' he said.

'No,' I said.

He studied my face intently as though for some reason he doubted the truth of what I had just said. Then he relaxed and said, 'No. No. How could you? There's only us.'

'Yes,' I agreed. 'There is only us.'

A short silence.

'Unless,' I added, 'there are other people in other Parts of the House. In Far Distant Places that you and I have not seen.

I have often wondered about that. As a hypothesis it is impossible to prove one way or the other – unless one day I come across signs of human activity, signs that cannot reasonably be attributed to our own Dead.'

'Mmmmm,' he said. He was deep in thought again.

Another silence.

It occurred to me that I might already have come across such signs. The fragments of paper with writing on them that I had found in the Eighty-Eighth Western Hall! They might belong to our own Dead or they might belong to Someone as yet unknown to us. I was about to tell the Other all about it when he began speaking again.

'Listen,' he said. 'I want you to promise me something.'

'Of course,' I said.

'If you ever see someone in the labyrinth – someone you don't know – I want you to promise me that you won't try to speak to them. Instead you must hide. Keep out of their way. Don't let them see you.'

'Oh, but think what an opportunity will be lost if I do that!' I said. 'The Sixteenth Person will almost certainly possess knowledge that we do not. He will be able to tell us about the Distant Regions of the World.'

The Other looked blank. 'What? What are you talking about? The sixteenth person?'

I explained about the Thirteen Dead and the Two Living, and how someone new would be the Sixteenth Person. (I have explained this many times. The Other can never seem to keep this important information in his head.)

'I agree that "the Sixteenth Person" is rather a cumbersome designation,' I said. 'We could, if you prefer, call him "16" for short. My point is that 16 has information about the World that we do not and therefore ... '

'No-no-no-no-no,' said the Other. 'You don't understand. It's really important that we keep as far away from this person as we can.' He paused and then said, 'You see, Piranesi, I've met this person. This person you call "16".'

'What? No!' I exclaimed. 'Then there really is a Sixteenth Person in the World? Why did you never tell me this before? This is wonderful! This is a cause for celebration!'

'No.' He shook his head dolefully. 'No, Piranesi. I know that this means a great deal to you and I'm sorry to have to break it to you. But this is not a cause for celebration. It's entirely the reverse. This person – 16 – means me harm. 16 is my enemy. And so, by extension, yours too.'

'Oh!' I said and fell silent.

What terrible news. Of course I understand the concept of enmity: there are many Statues in which one Figure struggles with Another. But I had never experienced it at first hand before. A random thought came to me – the phrase *kill him* on one of the scraps of paper from the Eighty-Eighth Western Hall. The person who had written that had had an enemy.

'Is there any possibility that you are mistaken?' I said. 'Perhaps it is all a misunderstanding. When 16 arrives, I can talk to him and explain that you are a Good Person with many Admirable Qualities. I can demonstrate to him that the attitude of hostility he holds towards you has no reasonable foundation.'

The Other smiled. 'How like you, Piranesi, to try and find the good in the situation. Unfortunately in this case it can't be done. This is why I didn't want to tell you about 16. You imagine that 16 can be reasoned with. But unfortunately, that's not the case. 16 is opposed to everything we are, everything you and I think is valuable and precious. And that includes reason. Reason is one of the things that 16 wants to tear down.'

'How dreadful!' I said.

'Yes.'

We lapsed into silence again. There seemed nothing more to say. I was shocked by his description of 16's wickedness. To be opposed to Reason itself!

After a moment the Other continued. 'But I'm probably stressing us both out for no reason. There's really only a very small likelihood of 16 coming here.'

'Why is the likelihood small?' I asked.

'16 doesn't know the way,' said the Other. He smiled at me. 'Try not to let it worry you.'

'I will try,' I said. A new thought struck me. 'When did you meet 16?'

'Mmm? Oh, the day before yesterday.'

'You have visited the Far-off Places where 16 lives? You never said so before. Tell me about them!'

'What do you mean?'

'You said you met 16. But you also said 16 does not know the way here. Meaning that you must have met him in his own Halls or, at any rate, in some Remote Region. This surprises me because I do not believe that you have undertaken any long journeys since I have known you.'

I smiled at the Other, awaiting his answer, which I fully expected would be very interesting.

He looked blank. Blank and slightly horrified.

A long silence.

'Actually … ' he began, then seemed to change his mind about what he was going to say. 'Actually, it's not important where we met. And I don't have time to go into all that now. I'm needed … I mean I can't stay today. I just wanted to warn you. You know, about 16.' Then he nodded briskly at me, picked up his shining devices and walked away towards the First Vestibule.

'Goodbye!' I called to his retreating back. 'Goodbye!'

I update my information about 16
ENTRY FOR THE TWENTY-SEVENTH DAY OF THE SIXTH MONTH IN THE YEAR THE ALBATROSS CAME TO THE SOUTH-WESTERN HALLS

I am very interested in the fact that the Other has met 16 and it is a great pity that he is so disinclined to say anything about it. I would like to know much more about the circumstances and location. But I suppose that the Other does not wish to dwell on a meeting with a wicked person.

The entry which I made in my Journal six weeks ago (See *A list of all the people who have ever lived and what is known of them*) is now outdated, so this morning I appended a note there directing the reader to this page.

The Sixteenth Person
The Sixteenth Person resides in a Far-off Region of the House, possibly in the North or South. I have never seen him, but the Other reports that he is a malevolent person, hostile to

Reason, Science and Happiness. The Other believes that 16 may attempt to come here in order to disrupt our Peaceful Existence and he has warned me that if I should ever see 16 in these Halls, I should hide Myself.

The First Vestibule
ENTRY FOR THE FIRST DAY OF THE SEVENTH MONTH IN THE YEAR
THE ALBATROSS CAME TO THE SOUTH-WESTERN HALLS

Today I decided to visit the First Vestibule. It is, oddly enough, a place I hardly ever go. I say 'oddly' because when I set up my System of Numbering the Halls several years ago I chose this Vestibule as the starting point, the place from which everything else is reckoned. Knowing Myself as I do, I do not think I would have chosen it had I not felt some sort of strong connection with it; yet I no longer remember what that connection was. (Is the Other right? Am I forgetting things? It is an unpleasant thought and I push it away.)

The First Vestibule is an impressive place, larger than the majority of Vestibules and more gloomy. It is dominated by eight massive Statues of Minotaurs, each one approximately nine metres high. They loom over the Pavement, darkening the Vestibule with their Bulk, their Massive Horns jutting into the Empty Air, their Animal Expressions solemn, inscrutable.

The temperature of the First Vestibule is different from that of the surrounding Halls. It is several degrees colder and there is a draught that blows from somewhere, bringing with it a smell of rain, metal and petrol. I have noticed this many times before, but somehow I always seem to forget about it immediately afterwards. Today I concentrated my attention on the scent. It was neither pleasant nor unpleasant, but extremely interesting. I followed its path. I passed along the Southern Wall of the Vestibule until I came to the two Minotaurs that flank the South-Eastern Corner. Here I noticed something. The Shadows between the two Statues were producing a sort of optical illusion. I could almost imagine that they extended backwards a long way and that I was in fact gazing into a corridor leading to a distant point where there was a patch of misty light. This patch of light contained other lights that seemed to flicker and move. It was from there that both the draught and the scent seemed to emanate. I could hear faint sounds – a sort of vibration and a dashing noise, like the Waves but less regular.

Suddenly I heard footsteps, followed by a voice, loud and indignant: ' ... not what I was hired to do and I said to him, "You have to be joking. You have to be fucking joking, mate."'

Another, glummer voice said: 'People have no shame. I mean what goes through their heads when ... ' The footsteps died away.

I leapt back from the South-Eastern Corner as if I had been stung.

What had just happened? Cautiously, I approached the Statues again and peered between them. The Shadows now looked unremarkable. I could sort of see how they might suggest the shape of a corridor, but that was all. The cold draught played around my ankles and I could still smell rain, metal and petrol, but the lights and the noises had vanished.

As I stood thinking of these things, four old crisp packets blew along the Pavement, one after the other. I made a sound of exasperation; this was a problem I thought I had dealt with. At one time I was forever finding crisp packets scattered about the First Vestibule. I also found old fish finger packets and sausage-roll wrappings. I gathered them up and burnt them so that they did not mar the Beauty of the House. (I do not know who it was that ate all the crisps and the fish fingers and the sausage rolls, but I cannot help wishing that he or she had been more tidy!) I also found a sleeping bag under the marble Sweep of the Staircase. It was very dirty and evil-smelling, but I washed it thoroughly and it has served me well.

I ran after the four crisp packets and picked them up. The fourth crisp packet was not a crisp packet at all. It was a crumpled-up piece of paper. I smoothed it out. On it was written the following:

All I am asking you to do is to give me directions to the statue you were telling me about — the one of an elderly fox teaching some young squirrels and other creatures. I would like to see it for myself. This task is not difficult and should be well within your capabilities. Write the directions in the space below. I have left a biro next to your lunch.

Eat it while it is hot — the lunch, not the biro.

Laurence

P.S. Please try to remember to take your multivitamin.

Underneath the message there was a large blank space for the recipient to write in but as it was still blank, I deduced that he or she had not given the writer the information they requested.

I would have liked to have kept the paper. It was evidence of two of the People who have lived: firstly, a person called Laurence and secondly, a person to whom Laurence had written and whose lunch and multivitamin he had provided. But who were they? I considered and immediately discounted the possibility that either of them was 16. The Other had said that 16 did not know the way here and clearly both Laurence and his friend had been familiar with these Halls at one time. They might well belong to my own Dead. But there was another possibility: that they were inhabitants of the Far-Distant Halls. If Laurence was still alive and waiting for the information about the Statue, then it would be wrong to take the paper.

I got out my own pen and wrote the following in the empty space.

Dear Laurence

The Statue of the Dog-Fox teaching two Squirrels and two Satyrs is in the Fourth Western Hall. From this Place go through the Western Door. In the next Hall go through the Third Door on the right. You will be in the First North-Western Hall. Follow the Southern (left-hand) Wall and again take the Third Door you come to. You will find yourself in a Corridor at the end of which is the Fourth Western Hall. The Statue is in the North-Western Corner. It is one of my favourites too!

1. *If you are alive then my hope is that you will find this letter and that the information I have given will be useful to you. Perhaps one day we will meet. You may find me in any of the Halls North, West and South of here. The Halls to the East are derelict.*

2. *If you are one of my own Dead (and if your Spirit passes through this Vestibule and reads this paper) then I hope you already know that I visit your Niche or Plinth regularly to talk with you and bring you offerings of food and drink.*

3. *If you are dead – but not one of my own Dead – then please know that I travel far and wide in the World. If ever I find your remains I will bring you offerings of food and drink. If it seems to me that no one living is caring for you then I will gather up your bones and bring them to my own Halls. I will put you in good order and lay you with my own Dead. Then you will not be alone.*

May the House in its Beauty shelter us both.

Your Friend

I placed the paper at the foot of one of the Minotaurs – the one nearest to the South-Eastern Corner of the Vestibule – and I weighted it down with a small pebble.

PART 3

THE PROPHET

The Prophet

From the Windows of the First North-Eastern Hall great shafts
of Light descended. Within one of the shafts a man was standing with his back to me. He was perfectly still. He was gazing
up at the Wall of Statues.

It was not the Other. He was thinner, and not quite so tall.
16!

I had come on him so suddenly. I had entered by one of the
Western Doors and there he was.

He turned to look at me. He did not move. He said nothing.

I did not run away. Instead I approached him. (Perhaps I was
wrong to do this, but it was already too late to hide, too late to
keep my promise to the Other.)

I walked slowly round him, taking him in. He was an old
man. His skin was dry and papery, and the veins were thick
and clotted in his hands. His eyes were large, dark and liquid,
with magnificently hooded eyelids and arched eyebrows. His
mouth was long and mobile, red and oddly wet. He wore a suit
in a Prince of Wales check. He must have been thin for a long
time because, although it was an old suit, it fitted him perfectly
– which is to say that it was wrinkled and saggy because the
fabric was old and worn, not because the cut was wrong.

I felt oddly disappointed; I had imagined that 16 would be
young like me.

'Hello,' I said. I was curious to hear what his voice sounded like.

'Good afternoon,' he said. 'If, in fact, it is afternoon where we are. I never know.' He had a haughty, drawling, old-fashioned way of speaking.

'You are 16,' I said. 'You are the Sixteenth Person.'

'I don't follow you, young man,' he said.

'There exist in the World two Living, thirteen Dead and now you,' I explained.

'Thirteen dead? How fascinating! No one ever told me there were human remains here. Who are they, I wonder?'

I described the Biscuit-Box Man, the Fish-Leather Man, the Concealed Person, the People of the Alcove and the Folded-Up Child.

'You know, it's the most extraordinary thing,' he said. 'But I remember that biscuit box. It used to stand on a little table next to the mugs in the corner of my study at the university. I wonder how it got here? Well, I can tell you this. One of your thirteen dead is almost certainly that dishy young Italian that Stan Ovenden was so keen on. What was his name?' He looked away, thought for a moment, shrugged. 'No, it's gone. And I imagine that another is Ovenden himself. He kept coming here to see the Italian. I told him he was asking for trouble, but he wouldn't listen. You know, guilt and so forth. And I wouldn't be surprised if one of the others is Sylvia D'Agostino. I never heard anything of her after the early nineties. As to who I am, young man, I can see how you might conclude that I am "16". But I am not. Charming as it is here … ' He glanced round. ' … I do not intend to stay. I am only passing through. Someone told me you were here. No,' He checked himself. 'That is not quite right. Someone told me what they thought had happened to you and *I* concluded you were here. This person showed me a photograph of you and since you were clearly a bit of a dish, I thought I would come and take a look at you. I'm glad I did. You must have been well worth looking at before, you know ... before everything happened. Ah, well! Old age happened to me. And this happened to you. And now look at us! But to return to the matter in hand. You mentioned two people living. I suppose the other one is Ketterley?'

'Ketterley?'

'Val Ketterley. Taller than you. Dark hair and eyes. Beard. Dark complexion. His mother was Spanish, you see.'

'You mean the Other?' I said.

'The other what?'

'The Other. The Not-Me.'

'Ha! Yes! I see what you mean. What an excellent name for him! The other. No matter what the situation he is only ever "the other". Someone else always takes precedence. He is always second fiddle. And he knows it. It eats him up. He was one of my students, you know. Oh, yes. Complete charlatan, of course. For all the grand intellectual manner and the dark, penetrating stare, he hasn't an original thought in his head. All his ideas are second-hand.' He paused a moment and then added, 'Actually all his ideas are mine. I was the greatest scholar of my generation. Perhaps of any generation. I theorised that this ... ' He opened his hands in a gesture intended to indicate the Hall, the House, Everything. ' ... existed. And it does. I theorised that there was a way to get here. And there is. And I came here and I sent others here. I kept everything secret. And I swore the others to secrecy too. I've never been very interested in what you might call morality, but I drew the line at bringing about the collapse of civilisation. Perhaps that was wrong. I don't know. I do have a rather sentimental streak.'

He fixed one bright, hooded, malevolent eye on me.

'We all paid a terrible price in the end. Mine was prison. Oh, yes. That shocks you, I imagine. I wish I could say that it was all due to a misunderstanding, but I did all the things they said I did. To be perfectly honest I did quite a lot more that they never knew about. Although – do you know? – I rather liked prison. One met such fascinating people.' He paused for a moment. 'Did Ketterley tell you how this world was made?' he asked.

'No, sir.'

'Would you like to know?'

'Very much, sir,' I said.

He looked gratified by my interest. 'Then I will tell you. It began when I was young, you see. I was always so much more brilliant than my peers. My first great insight happened when I realised how much humankind had lost. Once, men and women were able to turn themselves into eagles and fly immense distances. They communed with rivers and mountains and received wisdom from them. They felt the turning of the stars inside their own minds. My contemporaries did not understand this. They were all enamoured with the idea of progress and believed that whatever was new must be superior to what was old. As if merit was a function of chronology! But it seemed to me that the wisdom of the ancients could not have simply vanished. Nothing simply vanishes. It's not actually possible. I pictured it as a sort of energy flowing out of the world and I thought that this energy must be going somewhere. That was when I realised that there must be other places, other worlds. And so I set myself to find them.'

'And did you find any, sir?' I asked.

'I did. I found this one. This is what I call a Distributary World – it was created by ideas flowing out of another world. This world could not have existed unless that other world had existed first. Whether this world is still dependent on the continued existence of the first one, I don't know. It's all in the book I wrote. I don't suppose you happen to have read it?'

'No, sir.'

'Pity. It's terribly good. You'd like it.'

All the time that the old man was speaking, I was listening with great attention and trying to understand who he was. He had said that he was not 16, but I was not so naive as to believe him without further evidence. The Other had said that 16 was wicked, so it was possible that 16 would lie about who he was. But as the old man talked, I became more and more certain that he was telling the truth. He was not 16. My reasoning was this: the Other had described 16 as being opposed to Reason and to Scientific Discovery. This description did not fit the old man. The old man was as passionately fond of science as we were. He knew how the World was made and was eager to pass that knowledge on to me.

'Tell me,' he said, 'does Ketterley still think that the wisdom of the ancients is here?'

'Do you mean the Great and Secret Knowledge, sir?'

'Exactly that.'

'Yes.'

'And is he still searching for it?'

'Yes.'

'How amusing,' he said. 'He'll never find it. It's not here. It doesn't exist.'

'I was beginning to wonder if that might be the case,' I said.

'Then you are a good deal brighter than him. The idea that it's hidden here – I'm afraid he got that from me too. Before I had seen this world, I thought that the knowledge that created it would somehow still be here, lying about, ready to be picked up and claimed. Of course, as soon as I got here, I realised how ridiculous that was. Imagine water flowing underground. It flows through the same cracks year after year and it wears away at the stone. Millennia later you have a cave system. But what you don't have is the water that originally created it. That's long gone. Seeped away into the earth. Same thing here. But Ketterley is an egotist. He always thinks in terms of utility. He cannot imagine why anything should exist if he cannot make use of it.'

'Is that why there are Statues?' I asked.

'Is what why there are Statues?'

'Do the Statues exist because they embody the Ideas and Knowledge that flowed out of the other World into this one?'

'Oh! I never thought of that!' he said, pleased. 'What an intelligent observation. Yes, yes! I think that highly likely! Perhaps in some remote area of the labyrinth, statues of obsolete computers are coming into being as we speak!' He paused. 'I must not stay long. I am all too well aware of the consequences of lingering in this place: amnesia, total mental collapse, etcetera, etcetera. Though I must say that *you* are surprisingly coherent. Poor James Ritter could barely string a sentence together by the end and he wasn't here half as long as you. No, what I really came here to tell you is this.' He wrapped his cold, bony, papery hand round my hand; then he jerked me sharply towards him. He smelt of paper and ink, of a finely balanced perfume of violet and aniseed, and, beneath these scents, a faint but unmistakeable trace of something unclean, almost faecal. 'Someone is looking for you,' he said.

'16?' I asked.

'Remind me what you mean by that.'

'The Sixteenth Person.'

He put his head on one side to consider. 'Yeh-e-es ... Yes. Why not? Let us say that it is, in fact, "16".'

'But I thought that 16 was looking for the Other,' I said. '16 is the Other's enemy. That was what the Other said.'

'The other ... ? Ah, yes, Ketterley! No, no! 16 is not looking for Ketterley. You see what I mean about him being an egotist? Thinks everything's about him. No, it's you 16 is looking for. 16 has asked me how to find you. Now while I have no particular wish to oblige 16 — I have no particular wish to oblige anybody — I'm all in favour of doing Ketterley an ill turn. I hate him. He's spent the last twenty-five years slandering me to anyone who would listen. So I shall give 16 copious directions to get here. Minute instructions.'

'Sir, please do not do that,' I said. 'The Other says that 16 is a malevolent person.'

'Malevolent? I wouldn't say so. No more than most people. No, I'm sorry, but I simply must tell 16 the way. I want to put the cat among the pigeons and there's no better way to do it than to send 16 here. Of course, there's always the possibility – a very strong possibility really – that 16 will never get here. Very few people can come here unless someone shows them the way. In fact, the only person I ever knew who managed it – apart from myself – was Sylvia D'Agostino. She seemed to have a talent for slipping in between, if you follow me. Ketterley was absolutely dreadful at it, even after I had shown him numerous times. He could never get here without equipment – candles and uprights to represent a door and a ritual and all sorts of nonsense. Well, you saw all that when he brought you here, I suppose. Sylvia on the other hand could just slip away at any moment. Now you see her. Now you don't. Some animals have the facility. Cats. Birds. And I had a capuchin monkey in the early eighties who could find the way any time. I shall tell 16 the way and after that it all depends on how talented 16 is. What you need to remember is that Ketterley is afraid of 16. The closer 16 gets, the more dangerous Ketterley will become. In fact I shouldn't be at all surprised if he doesn't resort to violence of some kind. You might like to head off the danger by killing him or something.' (He pronounced 'off' as 'orrf'.) He smiled at me. 'I'm going now,' he said. 'We shan't meet again.'

'Then, sir, may your Paths be safe,' I said, 'your Floors unbroken and may the House fill your eyes with Beauty.'

He was silent for a moment. He seemed to contemplate my face and as he did so, a last thought occurred to him. 'You know I don't regret refusing to see you when you asked me before. That letter you wrote to me. I thought you sounded an arrogant little shit. You probably were then. But now … Charming. Quite charming.'

He picked up a raincoat that was lying in a heap on the Pavement. Then he walked in an unhurried manner to the Doorway leading to the Second Eastern Hall.

I consider the words of the Prophet
ENTRY FOR THE TWENTY-FIRST DAY OF THE SEVENTH MONTH IN THE YEAR THE ALBATROSS CAME TO THE SOUTH-WESTERN HALLS

Naturally I was very excited about this unexpected meeting. I went immediately and fetched this Journal and wrote it all down. I titled the entry *The Prophet*, because that is what he must have been. He explained the Creation of the World and told me other things that only a Prophet could have known.

I took time to study his words carefully. There was a great deal I did not understand though this, I expect, is usual with prophets, their minds being very great and their thoughts following strange paths.

I do not intend to stay. I am only passing through.

From this I understood that he inhabited Far Distant Halls and intended to return there immediately.

I can see how you might conclude that I am '16'. But I am not.

I had already determined this statement to be true. Perhaps (I hypothesised freely) the Prophet believed that the fifteen people who inhabited my Halls should be counted as one set of People, while in the Far Distant Halls there lived another set and he ought to be counted as one of them. Perhaps among his own People he was the Third Person or the Tenth. Perhaps he was even some dizzyingly high number like the Seventy-Fifth Person!

But I digress into what is surely fantasy.

I came here and I sent others here.

Could the Prophet have sent some of my own Dead to these Halls? The Fish-Leather Man or the Folded-Up Child? This was pure speculation. Like so many of the Prophet's statements, it remained, for the time being, impenetrable.

We all paid a terrible price in the end. Mine was prison.

I could make nothing of this.

… that dishy young Italian … Stan Ovenden … Sylvia D'Agostino … poor James Ritter …

The Prophet mentioned four names. Or, to be more accurate, three names and a designation ('that dishy young Italian'). This was a great addition to my knowledge of the World. If the Prophet had said no more than this, then his words would still have been priceless. The Prophet indicated that three of the names belonged to the Dead (Stan Ovenden, Sylvia D'Agostino and 'that dishy young Italian'). The status of 'poor James Ritter' was unclear to me. Did the Prophet mean that he was to be counted among the Dead too? Or was he one of the Prophet's own people in the Far Distant Halls? I could not tell.

So many questions! So many things I wished that I had asked him. But I did not reproach Myself. His appearance had been so sudden. I had been completely unprepared for it. Only now,

94

in solitude and peace, could I process the information he had given me.

... does Ketterley still think that the wisdom of the ancients is here? ... He'll never find it. It's not here. It doesn't exist.

I was delighted to have this confirmation that I was right. Perhaps it was a little conceited of me, but I could not help it. The consequences for my future work and collaboration with the Other I have yet to decide.

It was clear from many things the Prophet said that he and the Other had known each other at one time. The Prophet called the Other 'Ketterley' and said he was his student. Yet the Other has never spoken of the Prophet. I have talked to him on several occasions about the fifteen people the World contains, but he has never said to me, 'Fifteen is an incorrect number! I know of one more!' Which is strange (especially when you consider how much he likes to contradict me whenever an opportunity arises). But the Other has never been interested in finding out the number of people who have lived. It is one of the areas where our scientific interests diverge.

The closer 16 gets, the more dangerous Ketterley will become.

I have never known the Other show the least predisposition to violence.

You might like to head off the danger by killing him or something.

The Prophet, on the other hand, was clearly a violent person.

You know I don't regret refusing to see you when you asked me before. That letter you wrote to me. I thought you sounded an arrogant little shit. You probably were then.

This was the most baffling of all the Prophet's utterances. I never wrote him a letter. How could I when I only discovered yesterday that he existed? Perhaps one of the Dead wrote him a letter – Stan Ovenden or poor James Ritter – and the Prophet is confusing me with that person. Or perhaps prophets perceive Time differently from other people. Perhaps I will write him a letter in the future.

The Other describes the circumstances under which it will be right to kill me

ENTRY FOR THE TWENTY-FOURTH DAY OF THE SEVENTH MONTH IN THE YEAR THE ALBATROSS CAME TO THE SOUTH-WESTERN HALLS

Naturally I was anxious to tell the Other all about my meeting with the Prophet. It was vital that he know as soon as possible of the Prophet's intention to tell 16 the way to our Halls. Between Friday (the day I met the Prophet) and today (the day I was due to meet the Other) I looked everywhere for the Other, but I did not find him.

This morning I entered the Second South-Western Hall. The Other was already there and I saw immediately that he was in a state of some agitation. His hands were thrust into his pockets, he was pacing up and down and his face was dark with suppressed anger.

'I have something important to tell you,' I said.

He made a motion with his hand to brush away my utterance. 'It'll have to wait,' he said. 'I need to talk to you. There's something I haven't told you about 22.'

'Who?' I said.

'My enemy,' said the Other. 'The one who is coming here.'

'You mean 16?'

A pause.

'Oh, yes. Right. 16. I can't keep them straight, the bizarre names you give things. Well, there's something I haven't told you about 16. It's you that 16 is really interested in.'

'Yes!' I exclaimed. 'Strangely enough I already know. You see ... '

But the Other interrupted me. 'If 16 comes here,' he said, 'and I'm beginning to think now that it's a real possibility – then it'll be you that 16 will be looking for.'

'Yes, I know. But ... '

The Other shook his head. 'Piranesi! Listen to me! 16 will want to say things to you – things that you will not understand, but if you allow this to happen, if you allow 16 to speak to you, then those words will have a terrible effect. If you listen to what 16 says then the consequences will be awful. Madness. Terror. I've seen it happen before. 16 can unravel your thoughts just by speaking to you. 16 can make you doubt everything you see. 16 can make you doubt *me*.'

I was appalled. This was a level of wickedness that I had never imagined. It was frightening. 'How can I protect Myself?' I asked.

'By doing what I've already told you. By hiding. By not letting 16 see you. Above all by not listening to 16's words. I can't stress enough how absolutely vital that is. You have to understand that you're particularly vulnerable to this ... this power that 16 has, because you're already mentally unstable.'

'Mentally unstable?' I said. 'What do you mean?'

A flicker of annoyance crossed the Other's face. 'I told you,' he said. 'You forget things. You repeat yourself. We spoke about it a week ago. Don't tell me that you've forgotten already.'

'No, no,' I said. 'I have not forgotten.' I wondered whether to tell him my theory that it was he, not me, whose memory was at fault, but, what with one thing and another, now did not seem the time.

'Well, then,' said the Other. He sighed. 'There's more. There's something else I need to say and I want you to understand that this is as painful for me as it is for you. If I find that you've listened to 16 and that 16 has infected you with this madness, then that puts me at risk. You see that, don't you? There's a danger you might attack me. In fact it's very likely that you would. 16 will almost certainly try to manipulate you into hurting me.'

'Hurting you?'

'Yes.'

'How terrible.'

'Quite. And then there's the whole question of your dignity as a human being. You would be in this degraded, mad condition. It would be very humiliating for you. I can't imagine that you would want to go on like that, would you?'

'No,' I said. 'No, I do not think that I would.'

'Well,' he said and took a deep breath. 'In those circumstances, if I find you are mad, then I think it's best if I kill you. For both our sakes.'

'Oh!' I said. This was rather unexpected.

There was a short silence.

'But perhaps, given time and help, I might recover?' I suggested.

'It's unlikely,' said the Other. 'And in any case I really couldn't take the chance.'

'Oh,' I said.

There was a longer silence.

'How will you kill me?' I asked.

'You don't want to know that,' he said.

'No. I suppose not.'

'Don't think like that, Piranesi. Do what I've told you. Avoid 16 at all costs, then we won't have a problem.'

'Why have you not gone mad?' I asked.

'What?'

'You have spoken to 16. Why have you not gone mad?'

'I told you before. I have certain ways to protect myself. Besides,' he said with a rueful screwing up of his mouth, 'it's not as if I'm completely immune to it. God knows I feel half-mad with everything at the moment.'

We fell into silence again. We were both in a state of shock, I think. Then the Other put on a slightly forced smile and made an effort to appear more normal. A thought struck him. 'How did you know?' he asked.

'What?' I said.

'I thought you said … You seemed to be saying that you already knew that 16 was looking for you. You in particular. But how could you? How could you know that?' I could see by his face that he was trying to work it out.

Now was the time to tell him about the Prophet. It was on the tip of my tongue to do so. I hesitated. I said, 'It was revealed to me. By the House. You know how I have these revelations?'

'Oh. Right. That. And what was it that you wanted to say to me? You said you had something important to tell me.'

Another short pause.

'I saw an octopus swimming in the Lower Halls that are reached from the Eighteenth Vestibule,' I said.

'Oh,' said the Other. 'Did you? That's nice.'

'It was nice,' I agreed.

The Other took a deep breath. 'So! Keep away from 16! And don't go mad!' He smiled at me.

'You may be certain that I will keep away from 16,' I said. 'And I will not go mad.'

The Other clapped me on the shoulder. 'Excellent,' he said.

My reaction to the Other's declaration that he may, under certain circumstances, kill me
ENTRY FOR THE TWENTY-FIFTH DAY OF THE SEVENTH MONTH IN THE YEAR THE ALBATROSS CAME TO THE SOUTH-WESTERN HALLS

I had had a lucky escape! I had almost told the Other about the Prophet! And then he (the Other) would have said, 'Why did you speak to an Unknown Person when you promised me you would not? Did you not think that it might be 16?'

And what would I have answered? Because I *did* think that he was 16 when I spoke to him. I did break my promise to the Other. There is no excuse for it. Thank the House I had not told him! At best he would have thought me an untrustworthy person. At worst it would have inclined him all the more to kill me.

And yet I cannot help thinking that if the situation was reversed and if it were the Other's sanity that was threatened by 16, I would not resort to killing him quite so quickly. To be honest I do not think that I would ever want to kill him – the idea of it is abhorrent to me. Certainly I would try other things first, like finding a cure for his madness. But the Other is rather inflexible in his character. I would not go so far as to say it is a fault, but it is a definite tendency.

I change my appearance in anticipation of the coming of 16

ENTRY FOR THE FIRST DAY OF THE EIGHTH MONTH IN THE YEAR THE ALBATROSS CAME TO THE SOUTH-WESTERN HALLS

Just now I am practising hiding from 16.

Imagine, (I say to Myself) *that you have just seen someone – 16! – in the Twenty-Third South-Eastern Hall. Now hide Yourself!*

Then I run swiftly and silently to a Wall and I spring into the Gap between two Statues. I press Myself into it and remain still and silent. Yesterday a buzzard flew into the Hall where I was hiding, looking for smaller birds to eat. He circled the Hall and perched on the Statue of a Man and a Boy mapping Stars. He remained there for half an hour but did not perceive me.

My clothes are perfect for camouflage. When I was younger my shirts and trousers were different colours: blue, black, white, grey, olive brown. One shirt was a very nice cherry red colour. But they have all faded to mere ghosts of colours. All are now an undistinguished and indistinguishable grey, which fades into the greys and whites of the marble Statues.

However my hair is a different matter. Over the years, as it has grown longer, I have interlaced it with pretty things that I have found or made: seashells, coral beads, pearls, tiny pebbles and interesting fishbones. Many of these little ornaments are bright, shiny and have eye-catching colours. All of them rattle when I walk or run. So last week I spent an afternoon extricating them all. It was not easy and sometimes it was painful. I have placed my ornaments in the beautiful box with the octopus on it, which previously contained my shoes. When 16 returns to his own Halls, I shall put them back – I feel oddly naked without them.

The Index

ENTRY FOR THE EIGHTH DAY OF THE EIGHTH MONTH IN THE YEAR THE ALBATROSS CAME TO THE SOUTH-WESTERN HALLS

It is my practice to index my Journal entries every other week or so. I find that this is more efficient than indexing them straight away. After some time has passed it is easier to separate the important from the ephemeral.

This morning I sat down cross-legged on the Pavement of the Second Northern Hall with my Journal and Index. A great deal has happened since I last performed this task.

I made an entry in the Index:

Prophet, appearance of: Journal no. 10, pages 148–152

I made another entry:

Prophecies concerning the coming of 16: Journal no. 10, pages 151–152

Then I read over what the Prophet had said concerning the identities of the Dead and made an entry:

Dead, the, some tentative names for: Journal no. 10, pages 149, 152

I began to make entries for the individual names. Under the letter 'I', I wrote:

Italian, dishy, young: Journal no. 10, page 149

I was halfway through writing Stan Ovenden's name (under the letter O) when my eye was caught by an entry higher up.

Ovenden, Stanley, student of Laurence Arne-Sayles: Journal no. 21, page 154. See also The disappearance of Maurizio Giussani, Journal no. 21, pages 186–7

I was stunned. Here he was. Stanley Ovenden. Already in the Index. Yet his name, when the Prophet spoke it, had not been in the least familiar.

I read the index entry again.

I paused. I knew as I looked at it that there was something very strange here. But the strange thing was *so* strange, so entirely incomprehensible that I found it difficult to form coherent thoughts about it. I could see the strangeness with my eyes, but I could not think it with my mind.

Journal no. 21.

I had written Journal no. 21. Why in the World had I done that? It made no sense whatsoever. The Journal I am writing in now is (as I have already explained) Journal no. 10. There is no Journal no. 21. There never could have been a Journal no. 21. What did it mean?

I cast my eyes over the rest of the page. Most of the entries under O were about the Other. There were a great many of those, which is only to be expected seeing as he is the only other human being apart from Myself – and, of course, the Prophet and 16, but about them I know very little. I saw that there were earlier entries for other subjects. These were as strange as the entry for Stanley Ovenden. As I focussed on them, I experienced the same reluctance to register what my eyes saw. Nevertheless, I forced my eyes to see it; I forced my mind to think it.

Here were references to more Journals that did not exist! Journals 11, 17, 18 and 20. Journals 3 and 5 did exist of course, so those entries were sound. Except ... except ... The more I looked at them, the more I suspected that these entries did not refer to *my* Journals 3 and 5, but to different ones. The entries were written with a pen I did not recognise. The ink was thinner and more fluid and the nib of the pen was broader than any pen I possess. Added to this was the writing itself. It was my handwriting – no doubt about that – but it was subtly different from the writing I currently employ. It was slightly rounder and fatter – in a word, younger.

I went to the North-Eastern Corner and climbed up to the Statue of an Angel caught on a Rose Bush. I fetched out my brown leather messenger bag. I took all my Journals out of it. There were nine of them. Just nine. I did not find twenty others that I had inexplicably overlooked until this moment.

I examined the Journals carefully, paying particular attention to the covers and the numbers written on them. My Journals are black and I number each one with a white gel pen at the bottom of its spine. To my astonishment I discovered that the first three Journals had originally been numbered differently. They had been numbered 21, 22 and 23, but someone had scratched out the initial numeral '2', transforming them into 1, 2 and 3. The scratching out had not been done perfectly (gel ink is difficult to remove) and I could still make out the ghostly form of the '2'.

I sat for a while, trying to comprehend this, but I could make nothing of it.

If Journal no. 1 (my Journal no. 1) had originally been Journal no. *21*, then it ought to contain the two entries on Stanley Ovenden. I picked it up, opened it and turned to page 154. There he was. The entry was dated 22 January 2012. It was titled: *Biography of Stanley Ovenden.*

Stanley Ovenden. Born 1958, Nottingham, England. Father, Edward Francis Ovenden, owned a sweet shop. Mother's name and occupation unknown. Studied mathematics at the University of Birmingham. Began postgraduate research in 1981. The same year he attended one of Laurence Arne-Sayles's famous lectures: The Forgotten, the Liminal, the Transgressive and the Divine. *Shortly afterwards Ovenden abandoned mathematics and began a PhD in anthropology at the University of Manchester under Arne-Sayles's supervision.*

The first entry finished here, so next I turned to page 186, to the entry entitled: *The disappearance of Maurizio Giussani.*

In the summer of 1987 Laurence Arne-Sayles rented a farmhouse called the Casale del Pino, twenty kilometres from Perugia. His most favoured students (the inner circle) went with him: Ovenden, Bannerman, Hughes, Ketterley and D'Agostino.

Tensions had begun to appear within the group. Arne-Sayles had become highly sensitive to any remark or question that showed the speaker was insufficiently committed to his 'great experiment'. Anyone who dared to question him was subjected to a savage raking-over of all their failings, personal and academic. Consequently most of the group maintained a diplomatic silence, but Stanley Ovenden, who had a sort of tone-deafness when it came to other people's personalities, continued to express doubts about what they were doing. When Tali Hughes defended Ovenden to Arne-Sayles she also came in for a generous share of his spleen. The atmosphere at Casale del Pino became increasingly tense and, as a result, Ovenden and Hughes began spending more and more time away from the others. They became friendly with a young man, Maurizio Giussani, a philosophy student at the University of Perugia. This new friendship seems to have seriously alarmed Arne-Sayles.

On the evening of 26 July, Arne-Sayles invited Giussani and his fiancée, Elena Marietti, to a dinner party at Casale del Pino. During dinner Arne-Sayles talked about the other world (a place where architecture and oceans were muddled together) and how it was possible to get there. Elena Marietti thought that Arne-Sayles was talking metaphorically or else that he was describing some sort of Huxleyan psychedelic experience.

Marietti had to work the following day. (Like Giussani she was a postgrad student, but during the summer she worked as a paralegal in her father's law firm in Perugia.) At about 11 o'clock she said goodnight and got into her car and drove home and went to bed. The others were still talking. The English party had promised that one of them would drive Giussani home.

Maurizio Giussani was never seen again. Arne-Sayles claimed that he had gone to bed shortly after Marietti left and knew nothing about what had happened. The others (Ovenden, Bannerman, Hughes, Ketterley, D'Agostino) said that Giussani had refused the offer of a lift and that he had begun to walk home a little after midnight. (The night was moonlit and warm; Giussani lived about 3 kilometres away.)

Ten years later when Arne-Sayles was convicted of kidnapping another young man, the Italian police reopened the case of the missing Giussani, however ...

I stopped reading and stood up, breathing hard. I had a strong urge to fling the Journal away from me. The words on the page — (in my own writing!) — looked like words, but at the same time I knew they were meaningless. It was nonsense, gibberish! What meaning could words such as 'Birmingham' and 'Perugia' possibly have? None. There is nothing in the World that corresponds to them.

The Other was right after all. I had forgotten many things! Worse still, at the very point at which the Other has declared he will kill me if I become mad, I have discovered that I am mad already! Or, if not mad now, then certainly I have been mad in the past. I was mad when I wrote those entries!

I did not fling the Journal away. I dropped it on the Pavement and walked away. I wanted to put some physical distance between Myself and these evidences of my madness. The nonsense words — Perugia, Nottingham, university — echoed in my mind. I felt a great pressure there as if a whole host of half-formed ideas were about to break through into my consciousness, bringing with them more madness or else understanding.

I walked rapidly through several Halls, not knowing or caring where I went. Suddenly I saw in front of me the Statue of the Faun, the Statue that I love above all others. There was his calm, faintly smiling face; there was his forefinger gently pressed to his lips. In the past I have always thought he meant to warn me of something with that gesture: *Be careful!* But today it seemed to mean something quite different: *Hush! Be comforted!* I climbed up on to his Plinth and flung Myself into his Arms, wrapping my arm around his Neck, intertwining my

fingers with his Fingers. Safe in his embrace, I wept for my lost
Sanity. Great, heaving sobs rose up, almost painfully, from my
chest.

Hush! he told me. *Be comforted!*

I resolve to take better care of Myself

ENTRY FOR THE NINTH DAY OF THE EIGHTH MONTH IN THE YEAR
THE ALBATROSS CAME TO THE SOUTH-WESTERN HALLS

I left the Embrace of the Faun and wandered miserably through
the House. I believed that I was mad – or that I had been mad
– or else that I was becoming mad now. Whichever way it was,
it was a terrifying prospect.

After a while I decided that this way of going on did no good
at all.

I forced Myself to return to the Third Northern Hall
where I ate a little fish and drank some water. Then I revisited
all my favourite Statues: the Gorilla, the Young Boy playing
the Cymbals, the Woman carrying a Beehive, the Elephant
carrying a Castle, the Faun, the Two Kings playing Chess.
Their Beauty soothed me and took me out of Myself; their
noble expressions reminded me of all that is good in the
World.

This morning I am able to reflect more calmly on what has
happened.

I accept that I have been very ill in the past. I must have
been ill when I wrote those entries in my Journal or else I
would not have filled them with outlandish words such as
'Birmingham' and 'Perugia'. (Even now, as I write the words,

I begin to feel anxious again. A crowd of images stirs in my mind – strange, nightmarish, but at the same time oddly familiar. The word 'Birmingham', for example, brings with it a blare of noise, a flash of movement and colour and the fleeting image of towers and spires against a heavy grey sky. I try to catch hold of these impressions, to examine them further, but instantly they fade.)

Despite all this I believe that I was precipitate to dismiss these two entries as gibberish. Some of the words – 'university' is an example – do seem to possess meaning of a sort. I believe that if I set my mind to it, I could write a clear definition of 'university'. I have given some thought as to what might be the explanation of this. I understand 'scholar' because scattered around the House are Statues of Scholars with books and papers in their hands. Perhaps I extrapolated the idea of a 'university' (a place where scholars congregate) from these? This does not seem a very satisfactory hypothesis, but it is the best I can do for the moment.

The entries also include the names of people whose existence is confirmed by other evidence. The Prophet spoke about Stanley Ovenden, so clearly this was a real person. The Prophet also tried to think of the name of the dishy young Italian but could not do so. Perhaps it was Maurizio Giussani. Lastly both entries mentioned someone called 'Laurence Arne-Sayles' and I found a letter from 'Laurence' in the First Vestibule.

In other words, mixed in with the nonsense of these entries there does seem to be actual information. In my quest to learn all I can about the people who have lived I would be wrong to ignore this important source.

It has become clear that I have forgotten many things and — it is best to face these things squarely — I now have evidence of periods of serious mental derangement. My first and most important task is to hide these defects from the Other. (While I do not think he would go so far as to kill me because of them, he would certainly regard me with even more suspicion than he already does.) Almost as important is the need to guard Myself against the return of illness. To this end I have resolved to take better care of Myself. I must not become so absorbed in my scientific work that I forget to fish and end up with nothing to eat. (The House provides much food for the active and enterprising person. There is no excuse for going hungry!) I must devote more of my energies to mending my clothes and making coverings for my feet, which are often cold. (Question: is it possible to knit socks from seaweed? Doubtful.)

I have considered the renumbering of my Journals and have concluded that I must have done it Myself. Which means that twenty Journals (twenty!) are missing — a highly alarming thought! And yet, at the same time, it makes sense that there are missing Journals. I am (as I have previously stated) approximately thirty-five years of age. The ten Journals I possess cover a period of five years. Where are the Journals of my earlier life? And what did I do in those years?

Yesterday I thought that I never wanted to read or look up entries in my Journals again. I pictured Myself throwing all ten Journals and the Index into a raging Tide, and I imagined how relieved I would feel to be free of them. But today I am calmer. I am less at the mercy of fear and panic. Today I can see that there are sound reasons for studying my Journals carefully, even the mad parts – perhaps especially the mad parts. First, I have always longed to know more about the people who have lived and, incomprehensible as it is, the Journals do seem to contain actual information about them, however bizarrely presented. Second, I need to learn as much as I can about my own madness, specifically what triggers it and how I can guard against it in the future.

Perhaps by studying the past in the pages of my Journal I will be able to make sense of these things. In the meantime it is important to recognise that reading the Journal is in itself a triggering activity, giving rise to many painful emotions and nightmarish thoughts. I must proceed cautiously and only read small portions at a time.

The Other and the Prophet have both stated that the House itself is a source of madness and forgetfulness. They are scientists and men of intellect. When two such impeccable authorities are in agreement then I believe I must accept their conclusions. The House is the cause of my forgetting.

Do you trust the House? I ask Myself.

Yes, I answer Myself.

And if the House has made you forget, then it has done so for good reason.

But I do not understand the reason.

It does not matter that you do not understand the reason. You are the Beloved Child of the House. Be comforted.

And I am comforted.

Sylvia D'Agostino

I am very curious about the other people that the Prophet mentioned, so I decided to begin my study with Sylvia D'Agostino and poor James Ritter, but I did not look them up straightaway. In accordance with my plan of looking after Myself, I allowed a week and a half to elapse before I read the Journal again. I passed the intervening time in ordinary, soothing activities. I fished; I made soup; I washed clothes; I composed music on the flute that I made from the bone of a swan. Then this morning I brought my Journals and the Index to the Fifth Northern Hall. This Hall contains the Statue of the Gorilla and I thought the sight of Him would lend me Strength.

I sat down, cross-legged on the Pavement opposite the Gorilla. I turned to the letter D in my Index. There she was.

D'Agostino, Sylvia, student of Arne-Sayles: Journal no. 22, pages 6–9

I turned to page 6 of Journal no. 22 (which was my Journal no. 2).

Biography of Sylvia D'Agostino

Born 1958 in Leith, Scotland, the daughter of Eduardo D'Agostino, the poet.

Photographs show a woman of a slightly androgynous appearance, attractive, even beautiful, with thick dark brows, dark eyes, a strong nose and emphatic jawline. She had a mass of dark hair usually tied back. According to Angharad Scott, D'Agostino made no concessions to conventional ideas of femininity and only intermittently cared what she wore.

When she was a teenager D'Agostino told a friend that she wanted to go to university to study Death, Stars and Mathematics. Inexplicably the University of Manchester didn't offer such a course, so she settled for Mathematics. At the university she quickly stumbled upon Laurence Arne-Sayles and his lectures; that encounter shaped the remainder of her life.

Arne-Sayles's talk of communing with ancient minds and glimpses into other worlds answered all her cosmic longings – the 'Death and Stars' part of her. As soon as her Mathematics degree had concluded, she switched to Anthropology with Arne-Sayles as her supervisor.

Of all Arne-Sayles's students and acolytes D'Agostino was by far the most devoted. He assigned her a room in his house in Whalley Range where she became his unpaid housekeeper and secretary. She had a car (Arne-Sayles did not drive) and part of her duties consisted of driving him wherever he wanted to go, including to Canal Street on Saturday nights to pick up young men.

In 1984 she gained her doctorate. She did not seek out academic or teaching work, but stayed at Arne-Sayles's side, taking a string of menial jobs to support herself.

She was an only child and had always been very close to her parents, particularly her father. At some point in the mid-80s Arne-Sayles instructed her to quarrel with her parents. According to Angharad Scott, this was a test of loyalty. D'Agostino cut off all contact with her parents and they never saw her again.

Scott describes her as a poet, an artist and a film-maker and lists the magazines in which her poems were published: Arcturus, Torn Asunder and Grasshopper. (To date I haven't been able to find any copies of these magazines.) The editor of Grasshopper — a man called Tom Titchwell — was also a friend of Eduardo D'Agostino. He (Titchwell) kept in touch with Sylvia and relayed news of her back to her parents.

Two of her films survive: Moon/Wood and The Castle. Moon/Wood is a unique and atmospheric piece of film-making admired by critics and fans outside the usual circle of Arne-Sayles conspiracy theorists. It is 25 minutes long and was filmed on moors and in woods around Manchester. It was shot on Super 8 in colour, but the feel of it is almost entirely monochrome — black woods, white snow, grey sky etc. — with occasional splashes of blood-red. In the film a hierophant of ancient times holds a small community in thrall. He dispenses cruelty to the men and abuses the women. One woman opposes him. To show his power and to punish her, the hierophant casts a spell. The woman crosses a stream. She takes a step and her foot comes down in the moon's reflection. She is caught in the stream; she cannot move from the moon's reflection. The hierophant comes and beats her where she stands helpless. Still she cannot move. Left alone, she asks a wood of birch trees to help her. As the hierophant passes through the wood, he becomes caught in the tangle of birch trees; they bind him and pierce him. He cannot move and eventually dies. The woman is released from the moon's reflection. Moon/Wood contains very little speech and what there is is incomprehensible. The woman and the hierophant speak their own language which has nothing to do with ours. The true language of Moon/Wood is simple, stark imagery: moon, darkness, water, trees.

D'Agostino's other surviving film is even odder. It is untitled, but usually referred to as The Castle. It is shot on Betamax and the quality is very poor. The camera meanders around various enormous rooms, presumably in different castles or palaces (we cannot be seeing one building; it is simply too vast). The walls are lined with statues and puddles of water crowd the floor. According to the people who believe such things, this is a record of one of Arne-Sayles's other worlds, possibly the one described in his 2000 book, The Labyrinth. Other people have tried to establish the locations in order to prove that it is not a film of another world, but to date none of them has been conclusively identified. Notes in D'Agostino's handwriting were found with The Castle, but these are in the same peculiar code as her last diary and remain impenetrable.

D'Agostino seems to have kept a diary most of her adult life. The early volumes (1973–1980) were kept at her parents' house in Leith; these are written in English. Another diary, current at the time of her disappearance (spring 1990) was found in the doctor's surgery where she worked. This diary employs a weird mixture of hieroglyphs and descriptions of images (possibly dream imagery?) in English. Angharad Scott made several attempts to decipher it but got nowhere.

In early 1990 D'Agostino was working as a receptionist in a doctor's surgery in Whalley Range. She struck up a friendship with one of the doctors there, a man about her own age called Robert Allstead. At this point she seems to have been distinctly less enamoured of Laurence Arne-Sayles than before. She told Allstead that her life was one of drudgery, but that she would always be grateful to Arne-Sayles because he had opened the way to a more beautiful world and she was happy there. Allstead did not know what to make of this. He later told police that he was certain she was not on drugs. If she had been, he would never have allowed her to work in the surgery.

When Arne-Sayles learnt about her friendship with Allstead he threw one of his peculiar jealous fits and demanded that she leave the job. This time D'Agostino refused.

In the first week of April she failed to turn up for work. After she had been missing for two days Dr Allstead called the police. She was never seen again.

Poor James Ritter

SECOND ENTRY FOR THE TWENTIETH DAY OF THE EIGHTH MONTH IN THE YEAR THE ALBATROSS CAME TO THE SOUTH-WESTERN HALLS

There were two entries for James Ritter both in Journal no. 21: page 46 and page 122. The first one was titled: *The disgrace of Laurence Arne-Sayles.*

Arne-Sayles's career, always controversial, ended abruptly in April 1997, when a woman employed to clean his house found something: a brown liquid that seemed to ooze out from beneath a wall in one of the rooms. The room was a bedroom and, according to Arne-Sayles, not used. But the cleaner could see that it was being used, hence her cleaning it. She sponged up the liquid. Then she smelt it. Urine and faeces. A little more liquid seeped out from under the wall. She pushed the wall, it gave slightly. She put her ear to it. Then she called the police. Behind the wall — the fake wall — the police found a room in which was a young man, very ill and entirely incoherent.

Arne-Sayles's academic career was over. Following a trial (widely reported) he was sent to prison initially for three years; however, while in prison he was convicted of inciting other inmates to violence and riots. In the end he served four and a half years and was released in 2002.

Arne-Sayles did not testify at his trial and never offered any expla-
nation as to why he'd imprisoned James Ritter.

I found this entry to be disappointing; there was very little information as to who poor James Ritter was. I turned to the second entry. This looked more promising.

Biography of James Ritter

Born 1967 in London. In his youth Ritter was very good-looking. He worked as a model, a waiter, a barman, an actor and occasionally as a prostitute. Throughout his adult life he suffered prolonged periods of mental illness. He was sectioned at least twice between 1987 and 1994, once in London, once in Wakefield. He was sometimes homeless.

After he was found behind the fake wall in Arne-Sayles's house he was taken to hospital where he was treated for pneumonia, malnutrition, dehydration and bipolar disorder. The police tried to discover how long Arne-Sayles had kept him prisoner, but Ritter was incapable of giving any sort of coherent answer. So the police talked to people who knew him — drug addicts, social workers, people who ran hostels for the homeless. All that they (the police) were able to establish was that Ritter had been seen in and around Manchester in the early part of 1995, so it was possible — though by no means definite — that he had been imprisoned for as long as two years.

Ritter's own story, as he gradually became able to tell it, served to make matters more obscure. He insisted that he had only been at Arne-Sayles's house in Whalley Range for brief periods; most of the time he had been at a different house, a house that contained statues and where many of the rooms were flooded by the sea. Most of the time he appeared to think that he was still there. On several occasions while he was in hospital he became very agitated, saying that he needed to go back to the minotaurs because the minotaurs would have his dinner. Despite being put on medication to control his delusions, he continued to insist on this story of a house with a flooded basement and statues.

Quite what Arne-Sayles was trying to achieve by keeping Ritter prisoner is still a matter for debate. Two theories have been put forward.

The first is that Arne-Sayles brainwashed Ritter in order to lend credence to his claims that other worlds not only existed, but that he and other people had been there. Certainly, Ritter's description of the house is similar to the vast, empty rooms in Sylvia D'Agostino's film, The Castle; it is also similar to Arne-Sayles's own description of the other world in the book he wrote in prison: The Labyrinth. (Of course, it is perfectly possible that Arne-Sayles simply elaborated on Ritter's hallucinations.) But if that was Arne-Sayles's aim — to manufacture evidence of another world — then why did he choose a man with a history of delusional illness as his witness?

The second theory was that the kidnapping had less to do with Arne-Sayles's Other World theories than with his outré sexual tastes. (This was the line the prosecution took at the trial in October 1997.) But in that case why was Ritter babbling about houses with seas in the basement?

Angharad Scott attempted to interview Ritter for her biography of Arne-Sayles, but Ritter had taken offence that no one believed him about the house with the ocean imprisoned in it and he refused to speak to her. In 2010 a Guardian journalist — Lysander Weeks — tracked him down for a retrospective piece on the Arne-Sayles scandal. At this point Ritter was working as a caretaker for Manchester Town Hall. Weeks described him as calm, self-possessed, almost Zen-like. Ritter claimed to have been drug-free for a decade. Nevertheless the *story he told Weeks was the same one he had told the police: that for about eighteen months between 1995 and 1997 he had inhabited a large house where the sea flooded the basement and sometimes rose up to the ground floor. Ritter said he had slept in a sort of white, translucent cave beneath the marble sweep of a great staircase. Ritter said that working at Manchester Town Hall was what had saved him; it too was a vast building with great rooms and statues and staircases. The resemblance to the other house — the one Arne-Sayles had taken him to — calmed him.*

Journal entries on Sylvia D'Agostino and poor James Ritter: some initial thoughts

ENTRY FOR THE TWENTY-FIRST DAY OF THE EIGHTH MONTH IN THE YEAR THE ALBATROSS CAME TO THE SOUTH-WESTERN HALLS

The last entry on poor James Ritter was the one I found the most intriguing. It was just as full of nonsense words as the others, but the part about the Minotaurs was a clear reference to the First Vestibule. I also recognised Ritter's description of the white, translucent cave beneath a Staircase. The First Vestibule contains just such a Staircase with just such a cave-like space beneath it. And it was in that cave-like space that I had found much of the rubbish that had so annoyed me. James Ritter was clearly the person who had eaten crisps and fish fingers in the First Vestibule. (This insight alone justifies my decision to continue reading my Journal!)

Sylvia D'Agostino's entry was less informative, but judging by the description of her film, *The Castle*, she too had visited these Halls.

The word 'university' occurs three times in the entry about Sylvia D'Agostino and three times in the entries about Stanley Ovenden. Two weeks ago I hypothesised that I was able to ascribe a meaning to this seemingly nonsense word because I have seen Statues of Scholars in the House. At the time I was inclined to dismiss this theory as weak, but it seems more plausible now. It occurs to me that there are many other ideas that I understand perfectly, even though no such things exist in the World. For example I know that a garden is a place where one can refresh oneself with the sight of plants and trees. But a garden is not a thing that exists in the World nor is there any Statue representing that particular idea. (Indeed I cannot quite imagine what a Statue of a garden would look like.) Instead, scattered about the House are Statues in which People or Gods or Beasts are surrounded by Roses or Strands of Ivy, or shelter under the Canopies of Trees. In the Ninth Vestibule there is the Statue of a Gardener digging and in the Nineteenth South-Eastern Hall there is a Statue of a different Gardener pruning a Rose Bush. It is from these things that I deduce the idea of a *garden*. I do not believe this happens by accident. This is how the House places new ideas gently and naturally in the Minds of Men. This is how the House increases my understanding.

This realisation is very encouraging and I no longer feel quite so alarmed when a nonsensical word in my Journal gives rise to a mental image that I cannot account for. *Do not be anxious*, I tell Myself. *It is the House. It is the House enlarging your understanding.*

All the Journal entries contain names. I have made a list of those I have found so far. There are fifteen of them. Assuming that 'Ketterley' belongs to the Other and that another belongs to the Prophet, then thirteen remain. This is the exact number of the Dead in my Halls. A coincidence? After careful consideration I am inclined to think it might be. While fifteen people are *named*, several more seem to be implied in the text: people such as the friend to whom D'Agostino said that she wished to study 'Death, Stars and Mathematics'; 'the police' (who are mentioned in all the texts); the woman who cleaned Laurence Arne-Sayles's house; and the young men whom Laurence Arne-Sayles picked up on Saturday nights. It is impossible to say at this juncture how many of these people there are.

PART 4

16

I retrieve the scraps of paper from the Eighty-Eighth Western Hall

ENTRY FOR THE FIRST DAY OF THE NINTH MONTH IN THE YEAR
THE ALBATROSS CAME TO THE SOUTH-WESTERN HALLS

I had not forgotten the scraps of paper that I found in the Eighty-Eighth Western Hall, nor the ones that remained there, woven into herring gull nests.

Two days ago I gathered together supplies for the journey: food, blankets, a small saucepan in which to heat water and some rags. I set off and reached the Eighty-Eighth Western Hall about the middle of the afternoon. The gulls must have been out searching for food because there were none in the Hall, though fresh deposits of excrement on the Statues showed that it was still their roosting place.

Immediately I began work extricating the scraps of paper from the nests. The ease with which this could be accomplished varied. In some nests the seaweed was dry and fell apart at the first tug, but in others the paper scraps were cemented to the seaweed by the gulls' droppings. I made a fire using dry seaweed from the old nests; I heated water in the saucepan; then I dipped a rag into the water and applied it gently to the paper that was stuck in the nests. It was delicate work: too little hot water and the hard droppings would not soften; too much and the paper itself would dissolve. It took me many hours of labour, but by the evening of the second day I had recovered seventy-nine scraps from thirty-five nests. I examined every nest again and satisfied Myself that no more remained.

This morning I returned to my own Halls.

I spent some time trying to assemble the writing. Eventually, after an hour, I had part of a page – perhaps as much as half – and a few smaller sections of other pages.

The writing was very bad, full of crossings out. I read:

... that he has done to me. How could I have been so stupid? I will die here. There is no one coming to save me. I will die here. The silence [piece missing] *no sound, only the pounding of the sea in the rooms below. There is nothing to eat. I rely on him to bring me food and water – which only underlines my status as a prisoner, a slave. He leaves the food in the room with the minotaur statues. I indulge myself in long fantasies of killing him. In one of the destroyed rooms I found a jagged piece of marble about the size of a roof tile. I have thought about crushing his head with it. This would give me great satisfaction ...*

This was the writing of a very angry and unhappy person. I wondered who it had been? I wished that I could reach through his writing to comfort him, to show him the fish that abounds in every Vestibule, the beds of shellfish just waiting to be gathered, how with only a little foresight he need never go hungry, how the House provides for and protects its Children. I wondered about his persecutor, the man who had made him a slave. I felt very sad to think that there had existed such antagonism between two human beings, perhaps even between two of my own Dead. Had the Concealed Person tormented the Biscuit-Box Man? Or the other way round?

Very carefully I turned over the scraps and examined the reverse. The writing here was even worse.

I forget. I forget. Yesterday I could not think of the word for lamp-post. This morning I thought that one of the statues spoke to me. I passed some time (about half an hour I think) talking to it. I am LOSING MY MIND. How horrible, how terrible to be in this dreadful place and MAD. I am DETERMINED TO KILL him before this happens. Before I forget why I HATE HIM.

I sighed when I unravelled this. I took three envelopes the Other gave me once. In the first I placed the scraps that I had succeeded in putting together. On the outside of the envelope I carefully wrote a copy of the two transcriptions. In the second envelope I placed some scraps that fitted together, making fragments of sentences. In the third envelope I placed the scraps I had not managed to fit to any others.

A problem

ENTRY FOR THE SECOND DAY OF THE NINTH MONTH IN THE YEAR THE ALBATROSS CAME TO THE SOUTH-WESTERN HALLS

One overriding problem concerns me at the moment: whether or not to ask the Other about Stanley Ovenden, Sylvia D'Agostino, poor James Ritter and Maurizio Giussani. The Prophet called the Other 'Ketterley'. In the entry about the disappearance of Maurizio Giussani the name 'Ketterley' appears in close proximity to the names D'Agostino and Ovenden, and to Giussani itself. From this I conclude that the Other knew these people. I long to know more of them and several times it has been on the tip of my tongue to ask him. But always at the last moment I have hesitated. Supposing he said: *Where did you hear of these people? Who told you?*, I would not know what to say. He must not know that I have spoken to the Prophet. He must not know about the entries in my Journal.

He is full of suspicion. He thinks of nothing but the approach of 16. Two months ago he declared his intention to go to the One-Hundred-and-Ninety-Second Western Hall and perform the ritual, which he believes will summon the Great and Secret Knowledge, but at present all that is forgotten.

Lemon

ENTRY FOR THE FIFTH DAY OF THE NINTH MONTH IN THE YEAR
THE ALBATROSS CAME TO THE SOUTH-WESTERN HALLS

This morning I was on my way from the Third Northern Hall to the Sixteenth Vestibule. I passed out of the First Northern Hall and into the First Vestibule. I took a step or two, then stopped.

Something had just happened. What was it? What had just happened?

I took a couple of steps back into the Doorway and breathed in. There it was again! A scent. A perfume of lemons, geranium leaves, hyacinths and narcissi.

It was quite strong in this one spot. Someone – a person wearing a beautiful perfume – had stood for a while in the Doorway, perhaps looking out at the Long Vista of Receding Halls. I returned to the First Northern Hall but could find no trace of it there. I went back to the First Vestibule and passed southwards along the Wall under the looming Statue of a Minotaur. Yes, the scent was discernible here too. I traced the person's path as far as a point between the Doorway to the First Western Hall and the Doorway to the Corridor leading to the First South-Western Hall. There I lost it.

Who was the person who had passed this way? Not the Other. I knew the perfume he wore: a spicy scent of coriander, rose and sandalwood. The Prophet? I remembered his perfume very well. Again, quite different – violet had been the dominant note, with hints of cloves, blackcurrant and rose.

No, this was someone new.

16 had come. 16 was here.

My heart started beating faster. I looked around the Vestibule. The great space was darkened by the velvet Shadows of the Minotaurs with splinters of golden Light between. 16 did not step out from a hiding place to begin making me mad. Yet he had been there and perhaps no more than an hour before.

It was surprising to me that someone like 16, someone so wedded to Destruction and Madness, should wear a perfume so lovely, so redolent of Sunshine and Happiness. But then I told Myself that I was foolish to think like that. *Treat this as a warning*, I said. *Be on your guard. 16 will not wear his ill intentions in his face. It is very likely he will be pleasing to the eyes. His manners will be friendly and insinuating. That is how he intends to destroy you.*

More people to kill

ENTRY FOR THE SEVENTH DAY OF THE NINTH MONTH IN THE YEAR
THE ALBATROSS CAME TO THE SOUTH-WESTERN HALLS

This morning I told the Other about the perfume in the First Vestibule. To my surprise he took the news quite calmly.

'Yes, well, I'm beginning to think that it's better to get it over with,' he said, 'rather than hanging about, waiting for it to happen. And besides, perhaps it isn't such a bad thing after all.'

'But I thought you said that 16 is a great threat to us,' I said. 'I thought you said that he threatens your safety and my sanity?'

'That's true.'

'Then how can it possibly be good if he comes here?'

'Because the threat to us is so great that our only option is to eliminate 16 entirely.'

'How do we do that?'

For an answer, the Other put two fingers to his head in imitation of a gun and made the sound: *Boom!*

I was stunned. 'I do not think that I could kill someone however wicked they are,' I said. 'Even the wicked deserve Life. Or if they do not, then let the House take it from them. Not me.'

'You're probably right,' he said. 'I'm not sure I could kill someone with my hands.' He examined his own thoughtfully, spreading the fingers and turning them over. 'Though it would be interesting to try. Tell you what. I'll get a gun. That'll make it easier, whichever of us has to do it. Which reminds me, there's a possibility – a small possibility – that someone else might come here. If you ever see an old man ... '

' ... an old man?' I said, startled.

' ... yes, an old man. If you see him, tell me straightaway. He's not quite so tall as me. Very thin. Pale. With hooded eyes and a red, wet mouth.' The Other gave an involuntary shudder, then said, 'I don't know why I'm describing him to you. It's not as if hordes of old men are going to start turning up.'

'Why? Are you going to kill him as well?' I asked anxiously. I had no doubt that the Other was talking about the Prophet.

'Well, no,' he said. He paused. 'Although now that you mention it, it's about time that somebody did. It was always amazing to me that no one killed him while he was in prison. Anyway, tell me if you see him.'

I nodded in as non-committal a manner as I could manage. The Other had asked me to tell him if I saw the Prophet in the future, not if I had seen him in the past, so I was not exactly lying. The one good thing about this new development is that the Prophet has gone back to his own Halls and he said quite definitely that he did not intend to return.

I find writing made by 16
ENTRY FOR THE THIRTEENTH DAY OF THE NINTH MONTH IN THE YEAR THE ALBATROSS CAME TO THE SOUTH-WESTERN HALLS

For five days a steady, grey, drenching rain fell in all the Vestibules. The World was damp and chill and puddles formed on the Stone Pavements at the Doors to the Vestibules. The Halls were full of the chatter of birds who came there to shelter.

I kept as busy as I could. I mended my fishing nets and practised my music. But all the while at the back of my mind was the thought that 16 was here and intended to make me mad. I had no idea when the crisis would come, and it was not a pleasant feeling.

Today it stopped raining. The World became light of Heart again.

I made my way to the Sixth North-Western Hall, which is home to a flock of rooks. The moment they saw me they descended from their perches on the High Statues, wheeling and flapping and calling to each other. I scattered scraps of fish to feed them. Two alighted on my shoulders. One pecked at my ear, hoping to discover if I was good to eat. It made me laugh. Standing in the middle of the rattle and whirl of black wings, I was not paying attention to my surroundings and I did not at first see that on a Door to my right, there was a mark, a slash of bright yellow chalk. Then I did see it. I shrugged the birds away and went to look.

Long ago I used to mark Doors and Floors with chalk in this manner because I was afraid of losing my way. I had not done it for years, but as I looked at this yellow mark I thought at first that it must be one of my marks, which had somehow survived Flood, Tide, Wind, Rain, Mist. Yet at the same time I knew that I have never possessed any yellow chalk. I have some white chalk, some blue chalk and a small amount of pink chalk. But yellow chalk? No, I have never had such a thing.

Then I saw that on the Pavement by the Door were more chalk marks, this time in white.

Words! Not the Other's words. He rarely ventures this far from the First Vestibule. No, these were someone else's words. 16! I stood for a moment trying to take this in. This had never occurred to me: that 16 might leave written words to make people mad! (I had to applaud his ingenuity. I am not sure it would have occurred to me.)

But would they in fact make me mad? All the Other's warnings had been against my speaking to 16, against my listening

132

to him. Was it not probable that the danger resided in some quality of 16's voice? Perhaps the written word was safe? (I realised that the Other had been annoyingly unspecific.)

My eyes turned cautiously downwards. I read:

13TH ROOM FROM THE ENTRANCE. THE WAY BACK IS AS FOLLOWS. GO THROUGH THIS DOOR AND TURN LEFT IMMEDIATELY. GO THROUGH THE DOOR IN FRONT OF YOU AND THEN TURN RIGHT. KEEP TO THE RIGHT WALL. MISS TWO DOORS AND THEN …

Directions. It was only directions.

This did not seem too dangerous. I paused and examined Myself for signs of imminent madness or tendencies to self-destruction. Finding none, I read further.

They were directions from the Sixth North-Western Hall to the First Vestibule. Although the Path itself was somewhat meandering, the directions were clear, precise, efficient and the letters themselves square, upright and pleasing.

Using these directions, I traced 16's path back as far as the First Vestibule. Each Doorway I passed through was carefully marked with yellow chalk. The marks were somewhat below my eye-level. (I estimate that 16 is between 12 and 15 centimetres shorter than me.) Beneath each Doorframe he had written his directions again so that if any were destroyed by a Tide or a mishap, he would still have the others. How methodical he was!

I went to the Second Northern Hall and got some blue chalk. Then I returned to the Sixth North-Western Hall where

I had first seen 16's directions. (This seemed to be as far as he had gone.) Underneath his writing I wrote:

DEAR 16

THE OTHER HAS WARNED ME OF HOW YOU INTEND TO MAKE ME MAD. BUT IN ORDER TO MAKE ME MAD, YOU MUST FIRST FIND ME AND HOW WILL YOU DO THAT? THE ANSWER IS YOU WILL NOT. I KNOW EVERY NICHE OF THESE HALLS, EVERY APSE, EVERY PLACE TO HIDE. RETURN TO YOUR OWN HALLS, 16, AND REFLECT ON YOUR WICKEDNESS.

Writing this letter lessened the hunted feeling I had been experiencing. I felt much more in control of the situation – almost as much as 16. My only difficulty was that I did not know how to sign the letter. I could not write 'YOUR FRIEND' as I did when I wrote to the Other or to Laurence (the person who had wanted to see the Statue of an Elderly Fox teaching some Squirrels). 16 and I were not friends. I tried putting 'your enemy' but this seemed unnecessarily confrontational. I considered 'the one who will never submit to being driven mad by you' but that was rather long (and not a little pompous). In the end, I simply put:

PIRANESI

This being what the Other calls me.
(But I do not think that it is my name.)

I ask the Other about 16's writing

I met the Other this morning in the Second South-Western
Hall. He was wearing a suit of medium-grey wool and an
impeccable shirt of a darker grey. His mood was calm, serious and focussed. When I told him about the words that I had
found chalked on the Pavement of the Sixth North-Western
Hall, he simply nodded.

'Can 16 impart madness through the medium of the written word?' I asked. 'Ought I not to have read it?'

'16's words are dangerous whatever form they take,' he
said. 'It would've been better not to read it. But I don't blame
you. It took you by surprise. You weren't expecting a written
message. Quite frankly that hadn't occurred to me as a possibility either. But this is a critical time. We need to be more
careful.'

'I will be. I promise,' I said.

He gave my shoulder a couple of encouraging pats. 'There's
good news too,' he said, 'well, sort of. I've managed to get
hold of a gun. It was nowhere near as difficult as I thought it
would be. But – and this I suppose is the bad news ... ' He
made a rueful face. ' ... it turns out I'm a dreadful shot. I just
don't seem to be able to hit anything at all. I'll have to practice,
I suppose. Not quite sure how I'll manage that, but anyway ...
The thing is, Piranesi, try not to worry. One way or another
this nightmare will soon be over.'

'Oh, please!' I begged. 'Let us not kill 16!'

He laughed. 'And what's the alternative? To allow ourselves to be driven mad? I don't think so.'

I said, 'But when 16 sees his plan does not work, when he sees how we avoid him, he may return to his own Halls.'

The Other shook his head. 'There's not a chance of it, Piranesi. I know this person. 16 is relentless. 16 will keep on coming.'

Light in the Darkness
ENTRY FOR THE SEVENTEENTH DAY OF THE NINTH MONTH IN THE YEAR THE ALBATROSS CAME TO THE SOUTH-WESTERN HALLS

Three days passed. I kept watch for signs that 16 had been in our Halls, but I found none. Then in the middle of the third night I awoke suddenly. Something had woken me, but I did not know what it was.

I sat up. I looked around. The Stars blazed bright in all the Windows. The Thousand Statues of the Third Northern Hall, faintly lit by the Stars, looked out upon the Hall as if they blessed it. Everything was as it always was; and yet I could not rid Myself of the feeling that something was happening.

It was very cold. I put on my shoes and a woollen jumper, and I walked to the Second North-Western Hall. All was empty; all was quiet; all was peaceful.

I passed through a Door on my right into another Hall. Here I heard a faint sound. The sound repeated at irregular intervals and, as I walked on, it grew louder. It was like the distant bellow of an animal.

A faint blossoming of light emanated from a Door at the other end of the Hall. I had only just observed this when the light changed and brightened until it became a beam that sliced through the Darkness and illuminated the Statues on the Opposite Wall! Then, just as suddenly, it faded again.

I walked to the Door and peered inside.

There was someone in the next Hall – someone with a torch who was rapidly casting the beam from Wall to Wall, from Corner to Corner, searching the Darkness for something or someone. (This was the reason that the light had suddenly grown stronger and faded again.) The person was shouting: 'Raphael! Raphael! I know you're here!'

It was the Other.

'Raphael!' he shouted again.

Silence.

'You should never have come here!' he shouted.

Silence.

'I know every inch of this place! You can't escape! I'll find you in the end!'

Silence.

I slipped into the Hall, an action I performed with the utmost economy of movement. Nevertheless the Other must have glimpsed it out of the corner of his eye because he swung around and shone the torch on the Door I had just passed through, but he moved too suddenly, the torch jerked out of his hand and skittered across the Pavement. The light extinguished itself.

'Shit!' exclaimed the Other.

Darkness returned to the Hall. The Tides moved in the Halls below. The Other cast about, searching for his torch, muttering to himself.

My eyes, which had seen little when dazzled by the torch, began to adjust to the Starlight again. At first, I saw nothing but the quiet Hall, but then a flicker of movement passed along the Southern Wall, East to West. It was the merest suggestion of a grey shadow against the faintly gleaming Statues and I could almost have believed that I was imagining it. But I was not. It passed through a Door leading to the Fifth North-Western Hall.

16!

The Other had found the torch. He made it give out its beam again. Then he exited the Hall by one of the Northern Doors.

I waited until he had gone and then I ran rapidly, silently, after 16. I hid Myself in the Door to the Fifth North-Western Hall.

16 was standing in the Hall. Like the Other, he had a beam of light; but unlike the Other, he was not casting it around aimlessly. He shone it steadily on the Walls of the Hall. The strong, silvery white light illuminated the beautiful Statues and gave to each one a strange new shadow, so that the Walls appeared to be thickly covered in immense black feathers. 16 moved the torch slowly, making the feather-shadows elongate, shrink, swoop and spin. But as for 16 himself, I could see nothing of him. He was a mere blot behind the dazzle of the light.

16 contemplated the Statues for several minutes. Then he turned the light away from the Walls and walked to a Door that led to the Sixth North-Western Hall. He checked the Jamb to reassure himself that the chalk mark he had made was still there and he passed through. I followed and hid Myself in the next Doorway.

In the Sixth North-Western Hall, 16 was shining his torch on the message that I had written. He stood motionless for a long moment. I had told him to reflect on his wickedness. Was that what he was doing? Suddenly he knelt and began to write rapidly.

No one has ever written to me before.

16 wrote for a long time, which in some obscure way pleased me. But then I thought: *Why are you pleased? Why does it matter if the message is long or short? You know you may not read it. If you read it, you will go mad.* Part of me (a very foolish part) felt that it would almost be worth going mad in order to read the message.

The Darkness in front of 16 coalesced into two wild black shapes that flapped and beat the Air. Startled, 16 leapt up with a cry of alarm.

It was only two rooks who had been awakened by the unusual activity and had come to see what was happening.

'Piss off!' cried 16. 'Piss off! Go away! I'm busy!'

16's voice was not at all what I was expecting.

I departed as silently as I had come. I made my way back to the Third Northern Hall and lay down on my bed. But my mind was too full for sleep.

I erase a message from 16

As soon as the Sun rose I fetched my Index and my Journals. I opened the Index at R, but there was no entry for 'Raphael'.

I quickly ate some food and thanked the House for its Beneficence. I had a question that I needed to put to the Other but today was not one of the days when the Other and I meet, so I knew my question must wait.

I set off for the Sixth North-Western Hall. The rooks greeted me noisily, but I had no time to talk to them today. 16's message covered an area of the Pavement approximately 60 centimetres by 80 centimetres.

My heart beat fast in my chest. I glanced down:

I saw the words:

MY NAME IS …

I saw the words:

… LAURENCE ARNE-SAYLES …

I saw the words:

… ROOM WITH THE STATUES OF MINOTAURS …

What should I do? I knew that as long as the message existed I would experience a strong urge to read it. I decided that my only option was to destroy it.

I ran back to the Third Northern Hall and fetched an old shirt and some chalk. I say 'shirt'; in fact, the garment was so ragged that it scarcely deserved the name. I tore it in two. Then I ran back to the Sixth North-Western Hall. I tied one half of the shirt around my eyes as a blindfold. Holding the other half in my hand, I knelt down and began to sweep it over the surface of the Pavement, erasing 16's words.

After a couple of minutes, I removed the blindfold and looked. Bits of the message remained here and there.

                          COMPREHENSIBLE? MY
NAME
        LICE OFFI   READ THE FILES ON
YOUR DIS   IS VALENTINE
KETTER
                              RTAINLY
GROOMED OTHER POTENTIAL VICTIMS AND I
        A DISCIPLE OF THE OCCULTIST LAURENCE
ARNE-SAY
    NK HE KNOWS THAT I HAVE PENETRATED TH
           EN HERE FOR ALMOST SIX YEARS, DID YO
                     WAY OUT IS
LOCATE
           NED ME THAT YOU MAY BE SUFFERING
FROM

As none of this made much sense – at least at first glance – I was hopeful that it would not affect me. (So far I feel fine.) I knelt down and wrote a reply.

DEAR 16

AS LONG AS YOU REMAIN IN OUR HALLS THEN THE
OTHER WILL TRY TO KILL YOU. HE HAS A GUN!

I HAVE ERASED YOUR MESSAGE WITHOUT READING
IT. YOUR WORDS HAVE NOT TOUCHED ME. YOU HAVE
NOT MADE ME MAD. YOUR PLAN HAS FAILED.

PLEASE! RETURN TO THE FAR-DISTANT HALLS
WHENCE YOU CAME!

PIRANESI

I question the Other

ENTRY FOR THE EIGHTEENTH DAY OF THE NINTH MONTH IN THE
YEAR THE ALBATROSS CAME TO THE SOUTH-WESTERN HALLS

Today at ten o'clock I went to the Second South-Western Hall
to meet the Other.

He was standing by the Empty Plinth. He wore a suit of dark
brown wool and a shirt of dark olive. His gleaming shoes were
a chestnut colour.

'I want to ask you something,' I said.

'OK.'

'Why have you not been honest with me?'

The Other put on a cold look. 'I am always honest with
you,' he said.

'No,' I said. 'You are not. Why did you not tell me that 16
is a woman?'

The expression on the Other's face flickered from haughty denial, to irritation, to reluctant acquiescence in the space of about half a second. 'OK,' he conceded. 'I suppose that's fair enough. But I never said that she wasn't a woman.'

I rolled my eyes at this extraordinarily weak defence. 'I have been referring to 16 as "he" for months,' I said, 'and you have not corrected me – not once. Why not?'

The Other sighed. 'OK. The reason I didn't say anything is that I know you, Piranesi. You're a romantic. Oh, you talk about being a scientist and a disciple of reason – and most of the time you are. But you're also a romantic. I knew it was going to be hard enough as it was to convince you of the threat that 16 poses. But I thought it would be even harder once you knew she was woman. You would be so much more inter-ested in a woman. I thought you might even fall in love with her. I certainly didn't think you'd be able to stop yourself from talking to her. I know you may find this difficult to believe but I was actually looking out for you. It was so important that you didn't trust 16, because 16 is fundamentally untrustworthy. Do you see?'

There was a pause.

'Well,' I said. 'Thank you for looking out for me. I do not believe I would be so easily swayed in favour of a woman as you seem to suggest. Please do not keep things from me in future.'

'Fair enough,' said the Other. He frowned. 'Anyway, how did you know?' His voice became sharp with alarm. 'You haven't spoken to her, have you?'

'No. I saw her in the Sixth North-Western Hall and I heard her voice. She did not see me.'

'You heard her?' The Other was even more alarmed. 'Who was she speaking to?'

'The rooks.'

'Oh.' Pause. 'How bizarre.'

I decide to look up Laurence Arne-Sayles in the Index

ENTRY FOR THE NINETEENTH DAY OF THE NINTH MONTH IN THE YEAR THE ALBATROSS CAME TO THE SOUTH-WESTERN HALLS

The Other is right about one thing. I am not as rational as I thought. I used to smile (secretly) at the Other whenever I saw him acting out of self-love or arrogance or pride. My own actions were, I was sure, guided solely by Reason. But I was only deceiving Myself. A rational person would never have spoken to the Prophet in the First North-Eastern Hall. A rational person would have kept on cleaning the Pavement of the Sixth North-Western Hall until every trace of 16's message was erased.

It is not the fact 16 is a woman that fascinates and excites me – or at least, not entirely; it is the fact that she is another human being. I want to learn everything I can about her – or as much as I can learn without going mad. (That is the tricky part.)

I have not told the Other about the message that 16 wrote. Nor have I told him that after I erased it there were little half phrases and sentences remaining and that I left these untouched.

... IS VALENTINE KETTER(LEY) ... This refers to the Other. The Prophet said that the Other's name is Val Ketterley. It is not surprising that 16 writes about the Other since, according to the Other, 16 is obsessed with him and wants to destroy him.

… (CE)RTAINLY GROOMED OTHER POTENTIAL VICTIMS AND I … Is 16 boasting of her victims? Of the harm she has done and intends to do? Unclear.

… A DISCIPLE OF THE OCCULTIST LAURENCE ARNE-SAY(LES) … Everything keeps leading back to this one same person, Laurence Arne-Sayles, who I believe is identical with the Prophet.

… (BE)EN HERE FOR ALMOST SIX YEARS, DID YO(U) … Unclear what this refers to.

WAY OUT IS LOCATE(D) … A puzzling fragment. 16 appears to want to tell me about an exit. But I know these Halls, all their entrances and exits. She does not.

I have looked up 16 in my Index, using the name the Other called her. She is not there. So I shall look up Laurence Arne-Sayles.

Laurence Arne-Sayles

SECOND ENTRY FOR THE NINETEENTH DAY OF THE NINTH MONTH IN THE YEAR THE ALBATROSS CAME TO THE SOUTH-WESTERN HALLS

Once again I took my Index and Journals to the Fifth Northern Hall and sat down opposite the Statue of the Gorilla. May his Strength and Resolution give me courage! I opened the Index at A.

There were twenty-nine entries for Laurence Arne-Sayles. Some of these were only a line or two; others ran to several pages. I skim-read about half of them, but was no wiser. The information they contained varied wildly: lists of publications, biography, quotations, descriptions of people Arne-Sayles had met in prison. I came across one entitled: *Laurence Arne-Sayles: pros and cons of writing a book*, and, since the idea of writing a book appeals to me strongly, I read this with interest.

Possible project: a book about Arne-Sayles, exploring the idea of transgressive thinkers — people whose ideas go beyond what is thought acceptable within a discipline (or even possible). Heretics.

Not sure whether this is a good use of my time or not. Pros and cons.

- *Angharad Scott did a passable job with her book,* A Long Spoon: Laurence Arne-Sayles and His Circle. *(Con)*

- *That said, Scott's strength is biography, not analysis. She would be the first to admit this. (Pro? Neutral?)*

- *Scott herself is gracious, encouraging, willing to help. She would like to see another book written. Gave me quite a lot of background information and has indicated that there's more to come. See notes of phone call with Angharad Scott, page 153. (Pro)*

- *Arne-Sayles is quite a sexy subject? Major scandal, trial, prison sentence etc. (Pro)*

- *Arne-Sayles is the perfect example of a transgressive thinker — transgressive in more ways than one — morally, intellectually, sexually, criminally. (Pro)*

- *The extraordinary effect he had on his followers, getting them to believe that they had seen other worlds etc. (Pro)*

- *Arne-Sayles refuses to speak to academics/writers/ journalists. (Con)*

- *His close associates — the people who knew him at the time he claimed to be passing to and fro between this world and others — are few. Of that number several have disappeared and most of the others won't talk to journalists. (Con)*

- *Tali Hughes was the only student of Arne-Sayles's who was willing to talk to Angharad Scott. According to Scott, Hughes is emotionally unstable and possibly delusional. James Ritter spoke to a journalist (Lysander Weeks) in 2010. Might be worth a conversation? According to Weeks, Ritter works as a caretaker in Manchester Town Hall. Worth checking if Weeks himself is working on a book? (Neither pro nor con — neutral)*

- *Mystery of the people connected to Arne-Sayles who disappeared: Maurizio Giussani, Stanley Ovenden, Sylvia D'Agostino. (This is a strong pull for readers and therefore a definite pro. Unless I disappear myself, in which case, con.)*

- *Spending a long time writing about a deeply unpleasant man could be emotionally taxing. It's universally agreed that Arne-Sayles is malicious, vindictive, manipulative, spiteful, arrogant, a complete and utter prick. (Con)*

Not sure where this comes out. Very slightly con?

This told me very little about Laurence Arne-Sayles himself. It was the last entry of all that was the most informative. It was called:

Notes for a talk to be given at Torn and Blinded: a Festival of Alternative Ideas, Glastonbury, 24–27 May 2013

Laurence Arne-Sayles began with the idea that the Ancients had a different way of relating to the world, that they experienced it as something that interacted with them. When they observed the world, the world observed them back. If, for example, they travelled in a boat on a river, then the river was in some way aware of carrying them on its back and had in fact agreed to it. When they looked up to the stars, the constellations were not simply patterns enabling them to organise what they saw, they were vehicles of meaning, a never-ending flow of information. The world was constantly speaking to Ancient Man.

All of this was more or less within the bounds of conventional philosophical history, but where Arne-Sayles diverged from his peers was in his insistence that this dialogue between the Ancients and the world was not simply something that happened in their heads; it was something that happened in the actual world. The way the Ancients perceived the world was the way the world truly was. This gave them extraordinary influence and power. Reality was not only capable of taking part in a dialogue – intelligible and articulate – it was also persuadable. Nature was willing to bend to men's desires, to lend them its attributes. Seas could be parted, men could turn into birds and fly away, or into foxes and hide in dark woods, castles could be made out of clouds.

Eventually the Ancients ceased to speak and listen to the World. When this happened the World did not simply fall silent, it changed. Those aspects of the world that had been in constant communication with Men – whether you call them energies, powers, spirits, angels or demons – no longer had a place or a reason to stay and so they departed. There was, in Arne-Sayles's view, an actual, real disenchantment.

In his first published work on the subject (The Curlew's Cry, Allen & Unwin, 1969) Arne-Sayles said that these powers of the Ancients were irretrievably lost, but by the time he wrote his second book (What the Wind Has Taken, Allen & Unwin, 1976) he was not so sure. He had experimented with ritual magic and now thought it might be possible to get some of the powers back, providing you had a physical link with a person who had once possessed them. The best sort of link would be actual remains — the body or part of the body of the person in question.

In 1976 Manchester Museum had in its collection four preserved bog bodies, dated between 10 BCE and 200 CE, and named after the peat bog in which they had been found: Marepool in Cheshire. They were:

- Marepool I (a headless body)
- Marepool II (a complete body)
- Marepool III (a head, but not one that belonged to Marepool I)
- and Marepool IV (a second complete body).

Arne-Sayles was most interested in Marepool III, the head. Arne-Sayles said that he had performed a divination that had identified the head as belonging to a king and a seer. The knowledge the seer had possessed was exactly what Arne-Sayles needed to further his own researches. Combined with his own theories, it would result in a watershed moment for human understanding. In May 1976 Arne-Sayles wrote a letter to the director of the museum, asking to borrow the head so that he could perform a magical rite of his own invention, transfer the seer's knowledge to himself and so usher in a New Age for Mankind. To Arne-Sayles's astonishment, the director refused. In June Arne-Sayles persuaded fifty or so students to demonstrate outside the museum against this blinkered and outdated thinking. The students carried placards that said 'Free the Head'. Ten days later there was a second demonstration, during which a window was broken and there was a scuffle with the police. After this, Arne-Sayles seemed to lose interest in the bog bodies.

At the end of December the museum closed for Christmas. When it re-opened in the New Year, the staff discovered there had been a break-in. There was evidence of people having camped inside the museum. Food crumbs, biscuit packets and other litter were scattered about. There was a smell of cannabis. 'Free the Head' appeared again painted on a wall, and burnt stubs of candles were stuck to the floor. The candles formed a circle. Nothing appeared to have been taken but the cabinet in which Marepool III was displayed had been broken and the head had been handled. Some candle wax and fragments of mistletoe adhered to it.

The police and the museum staff naturally suspected Arne-Sayles. Arne-Sayles however had an alibi; he had spent the Midwinter festival with some wealthy neo-pagans at a farmhouse in Exmoor. The neo-pagans (people called Brooker) confirmed this. The Brookers revered Arne-Sayles as an extraordinary genius and a sort of pagan saint. The police did not think their testimony was reliable but had no means of refuting it.

No one was charged with the break-in at the museum, but in his next book (The Half-Seen Door, Allen & Unwin, 1979) Arne-Sayles talked about a Romano-British seer called Addedomarus who had been able to walk a path between worlds.

In 2001, while Laurence Arne-Sayles was in prison, a man called Tony Myers walked into a police station in London and asked to make a statement. He said that while a student at Manchester University he had broken into the museum on Christmas Day 1976. He had smashed a window, climbed in and then opened the doors to let other people in. He had witnessed Arne-Sayles performing a ritual with two other men. He thought that the two men were Valentine Ketterley and Robin Bannerman, but it was a long time ago and he could not be sure.

Myers said that at one point he had seen the lips of Marepool III move but he had not heard any words.

Myers was not prosecuted.

Arne-Sayles himself never wrote about the ritual he used with Marepool III. In the late seventies he was in any case changing his ideas. He was less concerned with the content of lost beliefs and powers and more interested in where they had gone. Based on his earlier idea that the lost beliefs and powers constituted a sort of energy, he said this energy could not have simply winked out of existence; it must have gone somewhere. This was the beginning of his most famous idea, the Theory of Other Worlds. Simply put, it said that when knowledge or power went out of this world it did two things: first, it created another place; and second, it left a hole, a door between this world where it had once existed and the new place it had made.

Picture it, said Arne-Sayles, like rainwater lying on a field. The next day the field is dry. Where has the rainwater gone? Some has evaporated into the air. Some has been drunk by plants and animals. But some has seeped down into the earth. This happens over and over again. For decades, centuries, millennia, the water, seeping down, makes a crack in the rock under the earth; then it wears the crack into a hole; then it wears the hole into a cave entrance – a kind of door in fact. Beyond the door the water keeps flowing and it hollows out caverns and carves out pillars. Somewhere, said Arne-Sayles, there must be a passage, a door between us and wherever magic had gone. It might be very small. It might not be entirely stable. Like the entrance to an underground cave it might be in danger of collapse. But it would be there. And if it was there, it was possible to find it.

In 1979 he published his third, most famous book, The Half-Seen Door, *in which he discussed these ideas of other worlds and described how, after a certain amount of struggle, he entered one of them.*

Extract from The Half-Seen Door *by Laurence Arne-Sayles*

Once you have found the door, it is always with you. You simply look for it and there it is. Finding it the first time is where the difficulty lies. Following the insights that Addedomarus had given me, what I eventually concluded was that it was necessary to cleanse one's vision in order to see the door. To do this one must return to the place, the geographical location where one last believed the world to be fluid, responsive to oneself. In short one must return to the last place in which one had stood before the iron hand of modern rationality gripped one's mind.

For me this was the garden of the house where I grew up in Lyme Regis. Unfortunately by 1979 the house had gone through several hands. The then-owners (dull exemplars of the prevailing mediocrity) were unsympathetic to my request to be allowed to stand in the garden for several hours performing an Ancient Celtic ritual. No matter. I discovered from a friendly milkman when they would be taking their holiday, returned at that time and 'broke in'.

The day I entered the garden was cold, rainy, grey. I stood on the lawn in the pouring rain, surrounded by the roses my mother had planted (though now forced to share their beds with flowers of insufferable vulgarity). Behind the rain were masses of colour — white, apricot, pink, gold and red.

I focussed on my memory of being a child in that garden, of the last time when both the world and my mind had been unfettered. I had stood before the roses in my blue wool romper suit. I gripped a metal soldier in my hand, his paint somewhat peeling.

To my surprise I discovered that the act of remembering was extremely potent. My mind was immediately freed, my vision cleansed. The long, complicated ritual that I had prepared became completely unnecessary. I no longer saw or felt the rain. I was standing in the clear, strong sunlight of early childhood. The colours of the roses were supernaturally bright.

All around me doors into other worlds began appearing but I knew the one I wanted, the one into which everything forgotten flows. The edges of that door were frayed and worn by the passage of old ideas leaving this world.

The door was perfectly visible now. It was in a gap between the Antoine Rivoire and the Coquette des Blanches. I stepped through.

I was standing in a vast chamber with stone floor and walls of marble. I was surrounded by eight massive statues, each one different, each depicting a minotaur. A great marble staircase rose up to a great height and descended to an equally disorientating depth. A strange thundering – as of a sea – filled my ears …

I remain calm

THIRD ENTRY FOR THE NINETEENTH DAY OF THE NINTH MONTH IN THE YEAR THE ALBATROSS CAME TO THE SOUTH-WESTERN HALLS

The description of Laurence Arne-Sayles's theories contained in my Journals corresponds closely to what the Prophet himself said. (More evidence that they are one and the same person!) I was pleased to rediscover the name Addedomarus, and to have its correct spelling. This was the name that the Other called on in his ritual three months ago! I feel certain that the Other learnt of Addedomarus from Laurence Arne-Sayles. ('All his ideas are mine,' the Prophet said.)

One sentence puzzles me: *The world was constantly speaking to Ancient Man.* I do not understand why this sentence is in the past tense. The World still speaks to me every day.

I believe I am better at reading these Journal entries than I was at first. I remain calm even when faced with the most obscure language. Words and phrases that pulsate with mysterious energy – words such as 'Manchester' and 'police station' – no longer discompose me. I seem, almost unconsciously, to have fallen into a habit of treating these entries as if they were the writings of an oracle or seer, someone in a frenzied or inspired state who imparts knowledge, albeit in a strange and not easily processed form.

Perhaps I was indeed in an altered state of consciousness when I wrote them? I find this theory persuasive, but it leaves several questions unanswered. What did I do to achieve this altered state? And why, when I have always thought of Myself as a scientist, did I begin this practice in the first place?

There will be a Great Flood

ENTRY FOR THE TWENTY-FIRST DAY OF THE NINTH MONTH IN THE YEAR THE ALBATROSS CAME TO THE SOUTH-WESTERN HALLS

One of my regular tasks is to maintain a Table of Tides. In order to do this I rely on my observations and on a set of equations that I have invented. Every few months I perform my calculations and make sure that there are no Extraordinary Occurrences in the coming weeks. I have been so occupied recently that I have rather neglected this work. This morning I sat down to apply Myself to it and immediately discovered something Highly Alarming – a Conjunction of Four Tides in less than a week's time!

I was shocked to think how close I had come to missing this event altogether! My last set of calculations were for a period that ended more than two weeks ago. I had neglected my duties and put Myself and the Other in mortal danger!

In my agitation I leapt up and walked rapidly up and down the Hall. *Oh, fuck! Fuck! Fuck! Fuck! Fuck!* I muttered to Myself. *Fuck! Fuck! Fuck! Fuck!* After a minute or two of walking uselessly to and fro, I spoke to Myself sternly, telling Myself that it was no good bewailing the Past; what was needed now was to plan for the Future.

I sat down again and set Myself to doing further calculations in order to understand more accurately what was likely to happen. Depending on the Force and Volume of the Waters – which are difficult to predict with exactness – between forty and a hundred Halls will be flooded.

Fortunately today was a Friday, one of the days when I have my regular meetings with the Other. I arrived in the Second South-Western Hall almost half an hour early, so anxious was I to speak with him.

The moment he appeared I said, 'I have something to tell you.'

He frowned and opened his mouth to protest; he does not like me to take charge of the meeting but on this occasion I overrode him. 'There will be a Great Flood!' I declared. 'If we do not prepare ourselves properly, there is a very real danger that we will be swept away and drowned.'

Immediately he was all attention. 'Drowned? When?'

'In six days' time. On Thursday. The Flood will begin to rise approximately half an hour before midday. A High Tide from the Eastern Halls will be followed by … '

'Thursday?' He relaxed again. 'Oh, that's OK. I won't be here on Thursday.'

'Where will you be?' I asked, surprised.

'Somewhere else,' he said. 'It's not important. Don't worry about it.'

'Oh, I see,' I said. 'Well, that is good. The Flood will be centred around a point 0.8 kilometres to the North-West of the First Vestibule. It is vital that you are out of the Path of the Waters.'

'I'll be fine,' said the Other. 'Will you be OK?'

'Oh, yes,' I said. 'Thanks for asking. I shall walk to the Southern Halls.'

'That's good.'

'That only leaves 16,' I said without thinking. 'I need to … ' I stopped. 'That is … ' I began and stopped again.

There was a pause.

'What?' said the Other, sharply. 'What are you talking about? What's any of this got to do with 16?'

'I only mean that 16 is not a native of these Halls,' I said. 'She will not know that a Great Flood is coming.'

'No, I suppose not. So what?'

'I do not want her to drown,' I said.

'Trust me, Piranesi. That would solve all sorts of problems. But, in any case, it doesn't really matter one way or the
other. You've no way of getting in contact with 16 and so you
couldn't warn her even if you wanted to.'

There was a silence.

'That's right, isn't it?' said the Other. 'You haven't spoken to
her?' He gave me a sharp, appraising look.

'I have not,' I said.

'Not now? Not in the past?'

'Not now. Not in the past.'

'Well, there you are then. Whatever happens it's not your
responsibility. I wouldn't worry about it.'

Another pause.

'Well,' said the Other at last. 'I expect you've got things to do.'

'Many things to do.'

'Preparing for this inundation and so forth.'

'Oh, yes.'

'Well, I'll leave you to it then.' He turned and walked
towards the First Vestibule.

'Goodbye,' I called. 'Goodbye!'

ARE YOU MATTHEW ROSE SORENSEN?
SECOND ENTRY FOR THE TWENTY-FIRST DAY OF THE NINTH
MONTH IN THE YEAR THE ALBATROSS CAME TO THE SOUTH-
WESTERN HALLS

My course of action was clear. I must go immediately to the
Sixth North-Western Hall and write a message to 16 warning
her of the coming Flood!

As I walked I thought about the last message I had left her – the one begging her to leave these Halls. Perhaps in the intervening time she had replied. Perhaps the reply would be something like:

Dear Piranesi
You are right. Today I will return to my own Halls.
Sincerely
16

If that was the case I could stop worrying about her drowning in the Flood.

But deep down I hoped that she had not gone back to her own Halls. Strange as it may seem, I knew that I would miss her if she had. Other than 16, there is only Myself and the Other in the World and (it may surprise you to read this) the Other is not always the best of company. I was looking forward to seeing if 16 had written me another message, even though I would not dare read it. I suppose that what I really hoped for was that she would write something like:

Dear Piranesi
Reading your useful and informative messages, I have come to realise
that if only I were to cast off my wickedness then we could be friends.
Let us meet and talk. I promise not to make you mad. In return will
you teach me how to be not-wicked?
Hopefully
16

I arrived at the Sixth North-Western Hall. The rooks greeted me noisily. On the Pavement I found the remnants of 16's last message and my own message. But there was nothing new. 16 had not written to me. I was disappointed, but I told Myself that this was only to be expected; if I kept erasing 16's messages without reading them it was hardly likely that she would keep writing.

I got out my chalk and knelt down. Beneath my last message I wrote:

DEAR 16

IN SIX DAYS' TIME A GREAT FLOOD WILL RISE IN THESE HALLS. EVERYWHERE WILL BE UNDER WATER TO A DEPTH GREATER THAN YOUR HEIGHT OR MINE.

ACCORDING TO MY ESTIMATIONS THE PERILOUS REGION WILL STRETCH AS FAR AS:

SIX HALLS WEST OF HERE

FOUR HALLS NORTH OF HERE

FIVE HALLS EAST OF HERE

SIX HALLS SOUTH OF HERE

THE FLOOD WILL LAST THREE TO FOUR HOURS AFTER WHICH IT WILL BEGIN TO SUBSIDE.

PLEASE ABSENT YOURSELF FROM THESE HALLS AT THIS TIME OR YOU WILL BE IN DANGER. THERE WILL BE <u>STRONG CURRENTS</u>. SHOULD YOU FIND YOURSELF CAUGHT BY THE FLOOD, THEN CLIMB

QUICKLY! THE STATUES ARE GRACIOUS AND WILL PROTECT YOU.

PIRANESI

I considered the message carefully. It was as clear as I could make it except for one thing. 'In six days' time' was only meaningful if 16 knew the day on which I had written the message and how would she know that?

I could write today's date, but that was according to a calendar of my own invention and it seemed unlikely that 16 had invented the same calendar as me.

POSTSCRIPT: TODAY IS THE SECOND DAY OF THE NEW MOON. THE DAY OF THE FLOOD WILL BE THE FIRST DAY OF THE QUARTER MOON.

All I could hope for was that 16 had not stopped visiting this Hall altogether and that she saw this warning.

Before the Flood comes I need to gather up all my plastic bowls – the ones I use to collect Fresh Water – so that they are not carried off by the Waters. I knew that there were two not far from the Sixth North-Western Hall, in the Eighteenth North-Western Hall on the other side of the Twenty-Fourth Vestibule. I thought I might as well get them now as I was in the Vicinity.

I walked to the Twenty-Fourth Vestibule. This Vestibule is notable for a shallow, sloping bank of white marble pebbles, which partially blocks the Mouth of the Staircase leading to the Lower Halls. The pebbles have been deposited here over time by the Tides. They have smooth, rounded shapes, delightful to the touch; they are a pure white colour with a beautiful, glowing translucency. I have climbed over this bank many times to fish and gather shellfish. Always I dislodge a few pebbles, but never so many that it alters the overall shape of the bank.

The first thing that I saw today was that some of the pebbles had been removed. There was a hollow in the side of the bank where no hollow had been before. I was astonished by this. Who could have done it? I have seen rooks and crows take small stones to break open shellfish, but birds do not move a great number of stones for no reason.

I looked around. Something white was scattered over the Pavement in the North-Eastern Corner of the Vestibule.

I approached. Too late I realised that the pebbles formed shapes. Words! Words made by 16! Before I had time to tear my eyes away I had read the entire message! In letters approximately 25 centimetres high it said:

ARE YOU MATTHEW ROSE SORENSEN?

Matthew Rose Sorensen. A name. Three words that make up a name.

Matthew Rose Sorensen …

An image rose up in front of me, like a memory or a vision.

… I seemed to be standing at the junction of many streets in a city. Dark rain poured down on me from a dark sky. Lights, lights, lights sparkled everywhere! The lights were many coloured and all were mirrored in the wet tarmac. Buildings rose up on every side.

Cars rushed past. Words and images were inscribed on the buildings.
Dark forms filled the streets; I thought at first that they were statues,
but they moved and I saw they were people. Thousands upon thou-
sands of people. More people than I had ever conceived of before. Too
many people. The mind could not contain the thought of so many.
And everything smelt of rain, and metal, and staleness. This vision
had a name and its name was ...

But, just as the word trembled on the brink of conscious
thought, it vanished and so too did the image. I was in the Real
World again.

I staggered and almost fell. I felt dizzy, parched, breathless.

I looked up at the Statues on the Walls of the Vestibule. 'I
need water,' I told them hoarsely. 'Bring me a drink of water.'

But they were only Statues and they could not bring
me water. They could only look down on me with Calm
Nobility.

I am ...

THIRD ENTRY FOR THE TWENTY-FIRST DAY OF THE NINTH MONTH
IN THE YEAR THE ALBATROSS CAME TO THE SOUTH-WESTERN
HALLS

16 had found a way to fulfil her dark purpose and make me
mad! I had erased her last message and what happened? She
had constructed a message I could not possibly erase without
reading it!

Are you Matthew Rose Sorensen?

I am ... I stuttered. *I am ...*

At first I could get no further than this.

I am ... I am the Beloved Child of the House.

Yes.

Immediately I felt calmer. Was any other identity even necessary? I did not think that it was. Another thought struck me.

I am Piranesi.

But I knew that I did not really believe this. Piranesi is not my name. (I am almost certain that Piranesi is not my name.)

I once asked the Other why he called me Piranesi.

He laughed in a slightly embarrassed way. *Oh, that* (he said). *Well, originally it was a sort of joke I suppose. I have to call you something. And it suits you. It's a name associated with labyrinths. You don't mind, do you? I'll stop if you don't like it.*

I do not mind, I said. *And, as you say, you have to call me something.*

The Silence of the House feels charged with expectation as I write these words. It seems to be waiting for something extraordinary to happen.

Are you Matthew Rose Sorensen?

How could I possibly answer this question when I had no idea who Matthew Rose Sorensen was? Perhaps the thing to do was to look up Matthew Rose Sorensen in the Index?

I went to the Eighteenth North-Western Hall and had a long drink of water. It was delicious and refreshing (it had been a Cloud only hours before). I rested a moment. Then I made my way to the Second Northern Hall where I fetched out my Index and Journals.

Are you Matthew Rose Sorensen?

The fact that Matthew Rose Sorensen had three names made him tricky to locate in the Index. I looked for him first under S. Nothing. I looked for him under R. There were three entries.

Rose Sorensen, Matthew: publications 2006–2010, Journal no. 21, page 6

Rose Sorensen, Matthew: publications 2011–12, Journal no. 22, pages 144–45

Rose Sorensen, Matthew, bio for Torn and Blinded: Journal no. 22, page 200

The last entry looked most promising.

Matthew Rose Sorensen is the English son of a half-Danish, half-Scottish father and a Ghanaian mother. He originally studied mathematics, but his interest soon migrated (via the philosophy of mathematics and the history of ideas) to his current field of study: transgressive thinking. He is writing a book about Laurence Arne-Sayles, a man who transgressed against science, against reason and against law.

I found it interesting that Matthew Rose Sorensen believed that Laurence Arne-Sayles had denied Science and Reason. In this he was not correct. The Prophet was a scientist and a lover of Reason. I spoke out loud to the Empty Air.

'I do not agree with you,' I said.

I was trying to summon up Matthew Rose Sorensen, to trick him into revealing himself. If he really was some forgotten part of Myself, then he would not like to be contradicted; he would argue his position.

But it did not work. He did not rise up from some shadowy recess of my mind. He remained an emptiness, a silence, an absence.

I turned to the other two entries.

The first was simply a list.

"'Now, here, now, always": J. B. Priestley's Time Plays', Tempus, Volume 6: 85–92

Embrace/Tolerate/Vilify/Destroy: How Academia treats Outsider Ideas, *Manchester University Press, 2008*

'Sources of outsider mathematics: Srinivasa Ramanujan and the Goddess', Intellectual History Quarterly, *Volume 25: 204–238,* Manchester University Press

The second entry was just more of the same.

'Timey-Wimey: Steven Moffat, Blink and J. W. Dunne's theories of Time', Journal of Space, Time and Everything, *Volume 64: 42–68, University of Minnesota Press*

"'The circles that you find in the windmills of your mind": The Importance of Labyrinths in Laurence Arne-Sayles's Exploitation of his Adherents', Review of Psychedelia and the Counterculture, *Volume 35, issue 4*

'The Gargoyle on the Cathedral Roof: Laurence Arne-Sayles and Academia', Intellectual History Quarterly, *Volume 28: 119–152, Manchester University Press*

Outsider Thinking: A Very Short Introduction, *OUP, pub. 31 May 2012*

'Time-travelling Architecture': article on Paul Enoch and Bradford for the Guardian, *28 July 2012*

I let out a long snort of frustration. This was utterly useless! Other than the fact that Matthew Rose Sorensen was interested in Laurence Arne-Sayles (which in no way differentiated him from everyone else in the World) I had learnt nothing. I felt a strong urge to shake my Journal, as if I could somehow shake more information out of it.

I sat for a long time thinking.

There was one person that I had not yet looked up in the Index and that was the Other. I had not thought of it until now. But perhaps if I read about the Other and found Matthew Rose Sorensen mentioned there, then ... I paused. Then what? Then perhaps I would be able to judge whether the Other knew Matthew Rose Sorensen, and ultimately whether Matthew Rose Sorensen was me.

There did not seem to be any harm in trying. In fact, of all the names in the World that I might look up, the Other seemed the safest. He and I had been friends for years. I opened the Index under O. I counted seventy-four entries for the Other. I had written far more about the Other than about any other subject. In fact, I had already been obliged to reallocate two pages from the letter P to accommodate them all.

I found:

Other, the, Rituals performed by
Other, the, Discourses on the Great and Secret Knowledge
Other, the, lends me a camera so that I can take pictures of the Drowned Halls
Other, the, asks me to make him a map of the Stars
Other, the, asks me to draw a map of the Halls immediately surrounding the First Vestibule

Other, the, proposes that the Statues form a sort of code, which we
might be able to decipher

and on and on and on. Until I reached the most recent
entries:

Other, the, uses the nonsense word 'Batter-Sea' to test my memory
Other, the, gives me a present of shoes

I skim-read a few entries. I read how the Other had
performed various Rituals at which I had assisted. I read how
clever the Other was, how scientific, how insightful, how
handsome. I read detailed descriptions of his clothes. This was
mildly interesting, but in no way helped me with my present
problem. Unlike the entries on Stanley Ovenden, Maurizio
Giussani, Sylvia D'Agostino and Laurence Arne-Sayles, none
of the entries on the Other was new to me. They contained
no arcane words or phrases that seemed to pulsate with
hidden meaning (words such as 'Whalley Range' and 'doctor's
surgery'). All the events were ones I remembered clearly. And
nowhere did the name Matthew Rose Sorensen appear.

I remembered that the Prophet had called the Other,
Ketterley. So I turned to K.

There were eight entries. The first was on page 187 of
Journal no. 2 (previously Journal no. 22).

Dr Valentine Andrew Ketterley. Born 1955 in Barcelona. Brought up
in Poole, Dorset. (The Ketterleys are an old Dorsetshire family.) Son of
Colonel Ranulph Andrew Ketterley, soldier and occultist.

Valentine Ketterley was a student of Laurence Arne-Sayles and
afterwards a research fellow in Social Anthropology at Manchester.

Married Clémence Hubert 1985. Divorced 1991. Two children. In 1992 Ketterley left Manchester and took up a teaching post at UCL. In June of the same year he wrote a letter to The Times *in which he publicly repudiated Arne-Sayles, accusing him of deliberately misleading and manipulating students, feeding them pseudo-mysticism and stories of other worlds. Ketterley called on the University of Manchester to dismiss Arne-Sayles. (The university did not do so until 1997 when Arne-Sayles was arrested for false imprisonment.)*

In recent years Ketterley has refused to answer any questions about Arne-Sayles.

Question: is it worth getting in touch with Ketterley to see if he will talk to me? Lives somewhere near Battersea Park.

Action point: make a list of questions for Dr Ketterley.

I was back on familiar ground. The entry was the usual mishmash of words that held a clear meaning and words whose meaning was obscure – always presuming that they meant anything at all. I noted with interest the re-emergence of the mysterious word 'Battersea' (and saw that it ought not to be hyphenated).

I returned to the Index to find the location of the next entry and it was then that I noticed something rather strange. The remaining entries – there were seven of them – were all on consecutive pages. The last ten pages of Journal no. 22 and the first thirty-two pages of Journal no. 23 were all about Ketterley.

I opened Journal no. 2 (previously Journal no. 22). The last ten pages – the very pages that I wanted – were missing; just a few torn edges remained in the spine. I opened Journal no. 3 (previously Journal no. 23) and found the same thing. The thirty-two pages with information about Ketterley were gone.

I sat back, mystified.

Who could have done this? Could it have been the Prophet? I knew that he detested Ketterley. Perhaps his hatred would cause him to destroy writing about his enemy? Or could it have been 16? 16 hated Reason. Perhaps she also hated Writing, a medium by which Reason can pass from one Person to another. But that made no sense. 16 had employed Writing to leave me a long message. And in any case how could the Prophet or 16 find my Journals? They are kept (as I have explained) in my messenger bag, which is hidden behind the Statue of an Angel caught on a Rose Bush in the North-Eastern Corner of the Second Northern Hall. It is one Statue among thousands, among millions. How would either of them know where to look?

I sat for a long time and thought. I had no recollection of tearing out the pages. But realistically who else could have done it? And I have known for some time that many things have happened of which I have no recollection. I have *done* many things of which I have no recollection (such as write these mysterious entries). Which meant I could have torn out the pages.

But if I had torn out the pages, what had happened to them? Where had they gone?

I fetched the scraps of paper that I found in the Eighty-Eighth Western Hall. I took out a few and spread them out so that I could examine them. One – a corner piece – bore the numeral 231. It was a page number from Journal no. 2.

Quickly – almost feverishly – I began to put the pieces together. There were approximately thirty entries covering a period that I had designated 15 November 2012 to 20 December 2012. The longest entry was titled: *The events of 15 November 2012*.

PART 5

VALENTINE KETTERLEY

The events of 15 November 2012

I visited him in mid-November. It was just after four, a cold blue twilight. The afternoon had been stormy and the lights of the cars were pixelated by rain; the pavements collaged with wet black leaves.

When I got to his house I heard music playing. A requiem. I waited for him to answer the door to an accompaniment of Berlioz.

The door opened.

'Dr Ketterley?' I said.

He was between fifty and sixty, tall and slender. A handsome man. He had an ascetic-looking head with high cheekbones and forehead. His hair and eyes were dark and his skin was olive-coloured. His hair was receding, but only a little, and he had a neatly trimmed, slightly pointed beard with more grey in it than his hair.

'Yes,' he said. 'And you are Matthew Rose Sorensen.'

I agreed that I was.

'Come in,' he said.

I remember how the smell of rain that pervaded the streets did not die away as I entered, but somehow intensified; inside the house there was a smell of rain, clouds and air, a smell of limitless space. A smell of the sea.

Which made no sense at all in a Victorian terraced house in Battersea.

He led me to a sitting room. The Berlioz was playing. He turned down the volume but it still played in the background of our conversation, the soundtrack of catastrophe.

I placed my messenger bag on the floor. He brought coffee.

'You're an academic, I understand,' I said.

'I *was* an academic,' he explained with a slight weariness. 'Until about fifteen years ago. I'm in private practice as a psychologist now. Academia was never very welcoming to me. I had the wrong sort of ideas and the wrong sort of friends.'

'I suppose the Arne-Sayles connection didn't do you any favours?'

'Well, quite. People still think I must have known about his crimes. I didn't.'

'Do you still see him?' I asked.

'God, no! Not for twenty years.' He looked at me speculatively. 'Have *you* spoken to Laurence?'

'No. I've written to him of course. But so far he's refused to see me.'

'Sounds about right.'

'I thought perhaps he didn't want to talk to me because he feels ashamed of the past,' I said.

Ketterley gave a short, sharp, humourless laugh. 'Hardly. Laurence has no shame. He's just perverse. If someone says white, he'll say black. If you say you want to see him, then he won't want to see you. That's just the way he is.'

I lifted my messenger bag on to my lap and fetched out my journal. As well as my current journal I also had with me the previous volume of my journal (which I referred to almost every day); the index to my journals; and a blank notebook that would form the next volume of my journal (I was very close to the end of the current one).

I opened my current journal and began to write.

He watched with interest. 'You use physical pen and paper?'

'I use a journal system for all my notes. I find that it's much the best way for keeping track of information.'

'And are you a good record keeper?' he asked. 'On the whole?'

'I'm an excellent record keeper. On the whole.'

'Interesting,' he said.

'Why? Do you want to offer me a job?' I asked.

He laughed. 'I don't know. Maybe.' He paused. 'What is it that you're actually after?'

I explained that I was chiefly interested in transgressive ideas, in the people who formulate them, and how they are received by the various disciplines – religion, art, literature, science, mathematics and so forth. 'And Laurence Arne-Sayles is the transgressive thinker *par excellence*. He crossed so many boundaries. He wrote about magic and pretended it was science. He convinced a group of highly intelligent people that there were other worlds and he could take them there. He was gay when it was still illegal. He kidnapped a man and to this day no one knows why.'

Ketterley said nothing. His face was a discouraging blank. He looked more bored than anything.

'I realise that all of this happened a long time ago,' I offered with a stab at empathy.

'I have an excellent memory,' he said coldly.

'Oh. Well, that's good. Just at the moment I'm trying to build up a picture of what it was like at Manchester in the first half of the eighties. Working with Arne-Sayles. What the atmosphere was like. What sort of things he was saying to you. What sort of possibilities he was conjuring up. That kind of thing.'

'Yes,' mused Ketterley, speaking apparently to himself, 'people always use words like that about Laurence. *Conjuring.*'

'You object to the word?'

'Of course I object to the fucking word,' he said irritably. 'You're suggesting that Laurence was some sort of stage magician and we were all his wide-eyed dupes. It wasn't like that at all. He liked you to argue with him. He liked you to put the rationalist point of view.'

'And then ... ?'

'And then he demolished you. His theories weren't just smoke and mirrors. Far from it. He'd thought everything through. It was perfectly coherent as far as it went. And he wasn't afraid to merge intellect with imagination. His description of the thinking of Pre-Modern Man was more persuasive than anything else I've come across.' He paused. 'I'm not saying that he wasn't manipulative. He was certainly that.'

'But I thought you just said ... ?'

'On a personal level. In his relationships he was manipulative. On an intellectual level he was honest, but on a personal level he was as manipulative as hell. Take Sylvia for example.'

'Sylvia D'Agostino?'

'Strange girl. Devoted to Laurence. She was an only child. Very close to her parents, particularly her father. She and her father were both gifted poets. Laurence told her to manufacture a quarrel with her parents and break off all contact with them. And she did. She did it because Laurence instructed her to do it and because Laurence was the great magus, the great seer who was about to guide us all into the next Age of Man. There was absolutely no advantage to him in cutting her off from her family. It didn't benefit him in the slightest. He did it because he could. He did it to cause anguish for her and her parents. He did it because he was cruel.'

'Sylvia D'Agostino was one of the people who disappeared,' I said.

'I don't know anything about that,' said Ketterley.

'I don't think you can claim he was intellectually honest. He said he'd been to other worlds. He said other people had been there too. That's not exactly honest, is it?' There may have been a slight edge of superciliousness in my voice, which I suppose I would have done better to suppress but I have always liked winning arguments.

Ketterley scowled. He seemed to struggle with something. He opened his mouth to say something, changed his mind, and then: 'I don't like you very much,' he said.

I laughed. 'I can live with that,' I said.

There was a silence.

'Why a labyrinth, do you suppose?' I asked.

'What d'you mean?'

'Why do you think he described the other world – the one he said he went to most often – as a labyrinth?'

Ketterley shrugged. 'A vision of cosmic grandeur, I suppose. A symbol of the mingled glory and horror of existence. No one gets out alive.'

'OK,' I said. 'But what I still don't quite understand was how he convinced you of its existence. The labyrinth-world, I mean.'

'He had us perform a ritual that was supposed to bring us there. There were aspects of the ritual that were ... evocative, I suppose. Suggestive.'

'A ritual? Really? I thought Arne-Sayles's position was that rituals were nonsense. Didn't he say something like that in *The Half-Seen Door*?'

'That's right. He claimed that he personally was able to access the labyrinth-world simply by making an adjustment to his frame of mind, by returning to a child-like state of wonder, a pre-rational consciousness. He claimed to be able to do this at will. Unsurprisingly, most of us – his students – got absolutely nowhere with this, so he created a ritual that we were to perform in order to access the labyrinth. But he made it clear that this was a concession to our lack of ability.'

'I see. Most of you?'

'What?'

'You said most of you couldn't enter the labyrinth without the ritual. It seemed to imply that some of you could.'

A slight pause.

'Sylvia. Sylvia thought she could get there in the same way that Laurence did. With this return to a state of wonder. She was a strange girl, as I've said. A poet. She lived very much inside her head. Who knows what she thought she saw.'

'And did you ever see it? The labyrinth?'

He considered. 'Mostly I had what you might call intimations, a sense of standing in a huge space – not just wide, but immensely tall too. And – this is quite hard to admit – but yes, I did see it once. I mean I thought I saw it once.'

'What did it look like?'

'Very much like Laurence's description. Like an infinite series of classical buildings knitted together.'

'And what do you think it meant?' I asked.

'Nothing. I don't think it meant anything at all.'

A short silence. Then he suddenly said, 'Does anyone know you're here?'

'Sorry?' I said. It seemed an odd question.

'You said that the Laurence Arne-Sayles connection dogged my career in academia. Yet here you are, an academic, asking questions about it all, dragging it all up again. I just wondered why you weren't being more careful. Aren't you afraid it will tarnish your brilliant career?'

'I don't think anyone is going to take issue with my approach,' I said. 'My book on Arne-Sayles is part of a wider project on transgressive thinking. As I think I've already explained.'

'Oh, I see,' he said. 'So you've told lots of people that you were coming here today to see me? All your friends.'

I frowned. 'No, I haven't told anyone. I don't usually tell people what I'm doing. But that's not because … '

'Interesting,' he said.

We looked at each other with a sort of mutual dislike. I was about to rise and go, when he suddenly said, 'Do you really want to understand Laurence and the hold he had over us?'

'Yes,' I said. 'Of course.'

'Then in that case we should perform the ritual.'

'The ritual?' I said.

'Yes.'

'The one to … '

'The one to open the path to the labyrinth. Yes.'

'What? Now?' I was a bit startled by the suggestion. (But I wasn't afraid. What was there to be afraid of?) 'You still remember it?' I said.

'Oh, yes. As I said, I have an excellent memory.'

'Oh, well, I … Will it take long?' I asked. 'Only I have to … '

'It takes twelve minutes,' he said.

'Oh! Oh, OK. Sure. Why not?' I said. I stood up. 'I don't have to take any drugs, do I?' I said. 'Because that's not really … '

He laughed that rather contemptuous laugh again. 'You've had a cup of coffee. I think that'll be sufficient.'

He lowered the blinds of the windows. He took a candle in a candlestick from the mantelpiece. The candlestick was an old-fashioned brass one with a square base. It didn't really match the rest of the furnishings in the house, which were modern, minimalist, European.

He got me to stand in the sitting room, facing the door that led to the hall. This area had been left free from furniture.

He picked up my messenger bag – the bag containing my journals, my index and my pens – and placed it on my shoulder.

'What's that for?' I asked, frowning.

'You're going to need your notebooks,' he said. 'You know. When you get to the labyrinth.'

He had an odd sense of humour.

(Writing this, I feel a sort of terror descend on me. I know now what is coming. My hand is shaking and I must stop writing for a moment to try to control it. But at the time I felt nothing, no presentiment of danger, nothing.)

He lit the candle and placed it on the floor of the hall, just beyond the door. The floor of the hall was the same as the floor of the sitting room: a solid wood flooring in oak. I noticed a blotch where he put the candlestick, as if the oak there had been repeatedly stained with candlewax, and within the dark stain was an unstained lighter square into which the candlestick base fitted precisely.

'You need to focus on the candle,' he said.

So I did.

But at the same time, I was thinking about that pale square in the dark patch and the candlestick fitting into it. And that was the point at which I realised that he was lying. The candle had stood in that precise spot many, many times and he had performed this ritual over and over again. He still believed. He still thought he could reach the other world.

I wasn't afraid, only incredulous and amused. And I started going over in my mind what questions I could ask him after the ritual in order to expose his dishonesty.

He turned out the lights in the house. It was dark except for the candle burning on the floor and the orange haze from the streetlights outside that penetrated the blinds.

He stood slightly behind me and instructed me to keep my eyes upon the candle. Then he began to chant in a language I'd never heard before. I surmised, from the similarities to Welsh and Cornish, that it was Brittonic. I think if I had not already found out his secret, I would have guessed it then. He chanted with conviction, with fervour, like he believed absolutely in what he was doing.

I heard the name 'Addedomarus' several times.

'Close your eyes now,' he said.

I did so.

More chanting. My amusement at discovering his secret sustained me for a while, but then I began to grow bored. He abandoned language altogether and seemed to drag out of himself a sort of animal growl that started in his stomach, impossibly deep, and grew higher, wilder, louder, more extraordinary.

Everything switched.

It was as if the world had somehow just stopped. He fell silent. The Berlioz was cut off mid-chorus. My eyelids were still closed but I could tell that the quality of the darkness had changed; it was greyer, cooler. The air felt colder and much damper, as if we'd been plunged into a fog. I wondered if somewhere a door had been thrown open; but that made no sense because at the same time the hum of London ceased. There was a sound of vast emptiness, and all around me waves were hitting walls with a dull thud. I opened my eyes.

The walls of a vast room rose up around me. Statues of minotaurs loomed over me, darkening the space with their bulk, their massive horns jutting into the empty air, their animal expressions solemn, inscrutable.

I turned in utter incredulity.

Ketterley was standing in his shirtsleeves. He was completely at his ease. He was looking at me and smiling as if I was an experiment that had gone surprisingly well.

'Forgive me for not saying anything before now,' he smiled, 'but I really am delighted to see you. A young, healthy man is just what I wanted.'

'Put it back!' I screamed at him.

He began to laugh.

And he laughed, and laughed, and laughed.

PART 6

WAVE

I was mistaken!

I was sitting cross-legged with my Journal in my lap and the fragments in front of me. I turned away slightly, not wanting to soil any of them, and vomited on the Pavement. I was shaking.

I fetched Myself a drink of water, as well as a rag and some more water to wipe up the vomit.

I was mistaken. The Other is not my friend. He has never been my friend. He is my enemy.

I was still shaking. I had the cup of water in my hand, but I could not hold it steady.

I had known once that the Other was my enemy. Or rather Matthew Rose Sorensen had known it. But when I had forgotten Matthew Rose Sorensen, I had forgotten this as well.

I had forgotten, but the Other remembered. I could see now that he was apprehensive in case one day I remembered. He called me Piranesi so he would not need to use the name Matthew Rose Sorensen. He tested me by speaking words such as 'Battersea' to see if they sparked any memories. I had been incorrect when I said that Battersea was nonsense. It was not nonsense. It was a word that meant something to Matthew Rose Sorensen.

But why was the Other able to remember when I was not?

Because he did not stay in the House but went back to the Other World.

Revelations came thick and fast now. My head seemed to shudder with the weight of them. I clasped my head in my hands and groaned.

I must not stay long, the Prophet had said, *I am all too well aware of the consequences of lingering in this place: amnesia, total mental collapse, etcetera, etcetera.* Like the Prophet, the Other never lingered. He never allowed our meetings to last longer than an hour and at the end of them he walked away; and when he did that he was walking away into the Other World.

But how could I make sure that I did not forget again? I pictured Myself forgetting and becoming the Other's friend again and running about the House taking measurements and photos and collecting data for him, while all the time he was laughing at me! No-no-no-no-no-no-no-no-no-no! I could not bear the thought of it! I pressed my head between my hands as if I could physically keep the memories from escaping.

I will learn from 16 and collect marble pebbles from the Vestibules and form letters with them. I will write in letters a metre high! *REMEMBER! THE OTHER IS NOT YOUR FRIEND! HE TRICKED MATTHEW ROSE SORENSEN INTO COMING INTO THIS WORLD FOR HIS OWN ADVANTAGE!* If necessary, I will fill Hall after Hall with immense writing!

... for his own advantage ... Yes, yes! That was the key to it. That was why he had brought Matthew Rose Sorensen here. The Other had needed someone — a slave! — to live in these Halls and collect information about them; he dares not do it himself in case the House makes him forget.

Furious, hot anger rose up inside me.

Why, why had I told him about the Flood? If only I had learnt all this before I knew about the Flood! Then I could have kept it a secret. I could have waited until Thursday came and I could have climbed up to a High Place, safe from the Waters and I could have watched him Destroyed. Yes! That is what I want now! Perhaps it is not too late! I will go back to the Other. I will smile and look as usual and I will deceive him as he has deceived me. I will say I made a mistake about the Flood. No Flood is coming. Be here on Thursday! Be in the very middle of these Halls!

But of course, the Other has said that he will not be here on Thursday. He is never here on Thursdays. He will be safe in the Other World. That does not matter! Anger makes me resourceful! On Tuesday the Other will come to meet me — it is our regular meeting day. I will snatch him and bind him with fishing nets. With these hands I will do it! I have two fishing nets. They are made of a synthetic polymer and very strong. I shall bind him to the Statues in the Second South-Western Hall. For two days he will be bound. He will be in torment, knowing the Flood is coming. Perhaps I will give him water to drink. Perhaps I will not. Perhaps I will say to him: 'Soon you will have plenty of Water!' And on Thursday he will watch the Tides pouring in through the Doors and he will scream and scream. And I will laugh and laugh. I will laugh as long and as loud as he laughed at Matthew Rose Sorensen when he brought him here …

This is where I lost Myself.

I lost Myself in long, sick fantasies of revenge. I did not think to rest. I did not think to eat. I did not think to drink water.

Hours passed — I do not how many. I wandered about and over and over in my imagination the Other died in the Flood or he fell from a great Height. And sometimes I raved at him and accused him; and sometimes I was cold and silent, and he begged me to tell him why I had turned against him, but I did not. And always I could have saved him, but I never did.

These imaginings left me ravaged. I do not think I could have felt more exhausted if I really had murdered someone a hundred times over. My thighs ached, my back ached, my head ached. My eyes and throat were sore with weeping and shouting.

When night came, I made my way back to the Third Northern Hall. I collapsed on my bed and slept.

It is 16 that is my friend and not the Other

ENTRY FOR THE TWENTY-SECOND DAY OF THE NINTH MONTH IN
THE YEAR THE ALBATROSS CAME TO THE SOUTH-WESTERN HALLS

I awoke this morning exhausted from the excesses of the day before. I went to the Ninth Vestibule to gather seaweed and mussels to make a broth for my breakfast. I felt dull and empty with no appetite for further anger. Yet, despite this emotional blankness, from time to time a sob or cry would escape my lips — a little sound of desolation.

I did not believe it was Myself that cried out. It was, I thought, Matthew Rose Sorensen who reposed in a state of unconsciousness somewhere inside Myself.

He had suffered. He had been alone with his enemy. It had been more than he could bear. Perhaps the Other had taunted him. Matthew Rose Sorensen had torn into pieces the description of his enslavement that he had written in his Journal and he had scattered the pieces in the Eighty-Eighth Western Hall. Then the House in its Mercy had caused him to fall asleep — which was by far the best thing for him — and it had placed him inside me.

But the sight of his name written in pebbles in the Twenty-Fourth Vestibule had caused him to stir uneasily and the revelation of what the Other had done had only made matters worse. I worried in case he woke up completely and his anguish began all over again.

I placed my hand on my chest. *Hush now!* I said, *Do not be afraid. You are safe. Go back to sleep. I will take care of us both.*

It seemed to me that Matthew Rose Sorensen fell asleep again.

I thought of all those Journal entries that I had read — the ones about Giussani, Ovenden, D'Agostino and poor James Ritter. I had thought that I was mad when I wrote them. But I could now see that this conclusion was incorrect. I had not written the entries at all; *he* had written them. And, what is more, he had written them in a different World where, no doubt, different Rules, Circumstances and Conditions applied. As far as I can tell, Matthew Rose Sorensen was in his right mind when he wrote them. Neither he nor I had ever been mad.

Another revelation came to me: it was the Other who wanted me to be mad, not 16. The Other had lied when he said 16 was trying to drive me insane.

I made my seaweed-and-mussel broth and drank it. It was important to keep up my strength. Then I took up my Journal again. I turned back to the message that 16 had written and which I had erased leaving only fragments.

IS VALENTINE
KETTER(LEY)
(CE)RTAINLY
GROOMED OTHER POTENTIAL VICTIMS AND I
    A DISCIPLE OF THE OCCULTIST LAURENCE
ARNE-SAY(LES)

I saw now that this whole passage was about Ketterley. The victims 16 talked about were not 16's own, but (most likely) Ketterley's. Had he tricked others into coming into this World? Or was Matthew Rose Sorensen the only victim? The word 'potential' suggested that 16 believed me to be the only one.

(THI)NK HE KNOWS THAT I HAVE PENETRATED TH(E)

This too referred to Ketterley. 16 was saying that Ketterley knew that she had arrived in these Halls. (Which he knew because I had told him. Inwardly I cursed my own stupidity.)

So why had 16 come?

Because she was looking for Matthew Rose Sorensen. Because she wanted to rescue him from the slavery of the Other. I saw it clearly now. It is 16 that is my friend and not the Other.

Tears sprang into my eyes at the thought. My only friend and I had hidden from her!

'I am here! I am here!' I shouted to the Empty Air. 'Come back! I will hide no longer!'

So many times I could have found her. I could have spoken to her that night when she knelt to write to me in the Sixth North-Western Hall. I could have waited by the trail of her perfume in the First Vestibule. Perhaps she had given up looking for me! Perhaps she had been disgusted when she saw how I hid from her, how I erased her message.

But no. She had formed that sentence in the Twenty-Fourth Vestibule: *ARE YOU MATTHEW ROSE SORENSEN?* It would have taken a long time to arrange those pebbles. 16 was patient, resolute and ingenious. 16 was still looking for me.

Perhaps by now she had found my message warning her of the Flood. Perhaps she had written something in return. I washed my bowl and the saucepan I had made my soup in; I put my possessions in order; then I set out for the Sixth North-Western Hall.

The rooks made a fuss at my approach. *Yes, yes. I am glad to see you too*, I told them. *Only I have things to do today and cannot stop for a long conversation.*

There was no new message from 16. But something very worrying had happened. My message warning her of the Flood had vanished. All our other messages were here, but not that one. I gazed at the empty Pavement in perplexity. What had happened? I know that I have forgotten many things; have I now started to remember things that have not happened? Had I, in fact, never written that message at all?

I passed from the Sixth North-Western Hall into the Twenty-Fourth Vestibule where 16 had constructed the message: *ARE YOU MATTHEW ROSE SORENSEN?* The pebbles that had formed the words were scattered far and wide over the Pavement. The words were utterly destroyed.

The Other. The Other had done this. I was quite sure of it.

I went back to the Sixth North-Western Hall and examined the Pavement carefully. I could see the faint traces of chalk where my warning had been. The Other had erased this message too.

Why?

He had scattered the pebbles in order to prevent me finding out about Matthew Rose Sorensen: that much was clear. But why erase the message to 16? In the hope that she would accidentally wander into the Perilous Region and be destroyed by the Flood? No. The Other does not hope; he plans and acts. He wanted her to drown and he would try to ensure it.

Three months ago, when the Other had first told me about 16, he said that he had spoken to her; but when I asked him where this conversation had taken place, he had become confused and would not tell me. That was because it had happened in the Other World, the existence of which the Other wanted to keep hidden from me.

The Other would contact 16 in the Other World and convince her to come to these Halls at the Hour of the Flood. Perhaps he had already done it. 16 was in danger.

I knelt down and quickly and efficiently restored the message the Other had erased. If 16 comes here between now and Thursday she will see the message and receive the warning of the Flood. And yet ... Only five days remain between now and Thursday. Supposing she does not come in this period? This seems to me perfectly possible; now that I know she comes from somewhere else (another World) it seems to me that her visits are irregular and unpredictable. There is a risk she will not see it and so I am in a state of some anxiety concerning her. My thoughts return constantly to her and her safety, yet I cannot think of anything else I can do to protect her.

Preparations for the Flood
ENTRY FOR THE TWENTY-SIXTH DAY OF THE NINTH MONTH IN THE
YEAR THE ALBATROSS CAME TO THE SOUTH-WESTERN HALLS

With the exception of the Concealed Person, all the Dead stand in the Path of the Flood Waters. On Sunday I began the work of carrying them to safety.

I took a blanket and transferred all the Biscuit-Box Man's bones into it – all except for the ones inside the biscuit box. I tied up the blanket with seaweed twine, making it into a sort of sack, and I carried it to the Second Vestibule and up the Staircase to the Upper Halls. There I emptied out the blanket and placed the bones on the Plinth of a Statue of a Shepherdess with a Lamb in her Arms. Then I went back for the biscuit box.

I did the same for the People of the Alcove and the Folded-Up Child, carrying each of them up a Staircase – whichever Staircase was nearest to their usual Habitation – and storing them carefully in one of the Upper Halls. I did not empty out the Fish-Leather Man but kept him wrapped up in the blanket (he has so many tiny fragments of bone that I am afraid of losing some). Similarly, I left the Folded-Up Child snuggled in a blanket, but that was more because I wanted her to feel safe in an unfamiliar Place.

It took me the best part of three days to complete the task. The bones of each individual Dead Person weigh between 2.5 and 4.5 kilograms and the Staircases are 25 metres high. Yet I found that it was good to do hard, physical work; it prevented me from continually obsessing over the injuries the Other has done me and my fears concerning 16.

I had not forgotten the albatross chick (now a very large bird!). I did a series of calculations to find out how the Forty-Third Vestibule would be affected by the flood and was relieved to discover that there would be, at most, only a thin skin of Water. The albatrosses consider me a friend, but I did not think they would allow me to carry their chick up a Staircase – and in any struggle between us they would surely win!

Yesterday was Tuesday, the day that I would normally go to my meeting with the Other. I did not go. Was he suspicious, I wonder? Or did he simply think that I was too busy preparing for the Flood?

The Statue of an Angel caught on a Rose Bush (behind which I keep my Journals and Index) is approximately 5 metres from the Floor; a height likely sufficient to keep them safe from the Flood. But, since my Journals and Index are almost as dear to me as my Life, I have placed them all in my brown leather messenger bag, wrapped the messenger bag in heavy-gauge plastic and carried it up to the Upper Halls and placed it beside the Biscuit-Box Man. I have stowed all my fishing gear, sleeping bags, pots and pans, bowls, spoons and other possessions in High Places out of the reach of the Flood. My last task was to gather up the remaining plastic bowls (the ones I use to collect Fresh Water).

I had just collected the last ones from the Fourteenth South-Western Hall and was carrying them back to the Third Northern Hall. On my way I passed through the First Western

Hall. This is the Hall that contains the Statues of the Horned Giants, those Vast Figures that emerge, struggling powerfully and with contorted Faces, from the Walls on either side of the Eastern Door.

I observed something near the North-Eastern Corner of the Hall and went to look at it. It was a bag made of some grey fabric and, lying beside it, two objects made of black canvas. The bag was approximately 80 centimetres long, 50 centimetres wide and 40 centimetres deep. It had two handles made of canvas, also grey. I picked it up; it was very heavy. I put it down again. It was fastened with two canvas straps that were held in place by metal buckles. I undid the buckles and opened the bag. I took out all the contents. They were as follows:

- a Gun
- a quantity of folded material made of a dense, heavy plastic. This was by far the largest object in the bag; it filled most of the bag and was coloured blue, black and grey.
- a small cylindrical container with a secure lid. This contained other small objects the purpose of which was unclear.
- a thing like a slice of a larger cylinder cut down at an angle, with a yellow hose coming out of it
- two black plastic rods extendable to a length of approximately 2 metres
- 4 black paddle-shapes

After studying these items for a minute or two I saw that the paddle-shapes could be attached to the ends of the black rods. I unfolded the material; it became a long flat shape, which was pointed at both ends. It was a boat. The thing like a slice of a cylinder was a bellows or pump. You pumped Air into the long flat shape and it would inflate and become a boat about 4 metres long and 1 metre wide.

I examined the two black canvas objects that had lain beside the bag. They had a number of straps hanging from them. I concluded that they must belong to the boat, but beyond this I could not ascertain their purpose.

Why had a boat appeared suddenly in the House on the eve of the Flood? Had the House sent it to me to keep me safe? I considered this proposition. There had been other Floods in the past and no boat had appeared; also, although I could imagine that the House might send me a boat, I could not imagine any circumstances in which it would send me a Gun. No, the Gun proclaimed the bag's ownership; it was the Other's.

I folded up the boat and packed everything neatly back in the bag. Everything except the Gun. I picked it up and held it for some time, thinking. I could take it and descend the Great Staircase in the First Vestibule to the Lower Halls. I could throw it into the Tides.

I replaced the Gun in the bag and did up the closures. I returned to the Third Northern Hall.

Wave

ENTRY FOR THE TWENTY-SEVENTH DAY OF THE NINTH MONTH IN THE YEAR THE ALBATROSS CAME TO THE SOUTH-WESTERN HALLS

Today was the day of the Flood. I woke at my usual time. I was keyed up with nerves and my stomach was clenched tight.

The day felt cold and I could tell by the touch of the Air on my skin that it was already raining in the Vestibules.

I had no appetite, but nevertheless I heated a little soup and forced Myself to drink it. It is important to keep the body well nourished. I washed up my pan and bowl and stowed the last of my possessions behind High Statues. I put on my watch.

It was a quarter to eight.

My most important task was to find 16 and ensure her safety. But as to the best way to accomplish it, that was far from clear. I was certain that the Other had set a trap for 16. Most likely he had promised to meet her in a certain Hall at a certain time and to tell her how to find Matthew Rose Sorensen. This meant that the most reliable way to find 16 was to look for the Other, but I did not want to go near the Other if I could avoid it. I remembered the words of the Prophet:

The closer 16 gets, the more dangerous Ketterley will become.

My hope was that I could find 16 before she reached the Other.

I went to the First Vestibule. I stood in the grey Rain and waited, hoping that she would appear. Between nine o'clock and ten o'clock I searched the adjacent Halls. Nothing. At ten o'clock I returned to the First Vestibule.

At half-past ten I began to walk between the First Vestibule and the Sixth North-Western Hall; I followed the Path laid down in 16's directions. I trod this Path six times, but I did not find her. I was growing extremely anxious.

I returned to the First Vestibule. It was now half-past eleven. Two Halls West and North of here, in the Ninth Vestibule, the first Tide was already ascending the Easternmost Staircase. A delicate Wash of Water was scuttling over the Pavements of the surrounding Halls.

There was nothing for it. I must look for the Other. I had only just come to this decision, when upon the instant he appeared in front of me. (Why could 16 not do that?) He walked briskly across the First Vestibule, East to West. His head was ducked down against the Rain. His clothes were strikingly different from what he usually wore: jeans, an old jumper and sneakers, and over his jumper an odd sort of harness. *Life-jacket*, I thought. (Or rather Matthew Rose Sorensen thought it inside my head.)

He did not see me. He passed into the First Western Hall. Silently I followed him and hid Myself in a Niche near the Door.

The Other went immediately to the bag containing the inflatable boat and began to unpack it. I waited, watching constantly for 16. The Other's attention was elsewhere and there might still be enough time to intercept her if she entered the Hall.

Some distance behind the Other, at the Western End of the Hall, I could see the glitter of Light on the Pavement: a film of Water was washing through the North-Western Doors. I glanced at my watch. Five Halls South and West of here, in the Twenty-Second Vestibule, another Tide was already rising, tumbling up the Staircase.

The Other unrolled his boat. He attached his little pump to it and began to pump with his foot. The boat began to inflate in an efficient manner.

Water was filling up the Second and Third South-Western Halls; I could hear the dull thud of the Waves hitting their Walls.

Then it came to me. 16 was clever. She was at least as clever as me, perhaps even more so. She knew nothing about the Flood but she would not trust the Other. She would wait and watch, as I was doing, hoping that Matthew Rose Sorensen would appear. Suddenly I had a mental image of both 16 and Myself hiding in the First Western Hall, both waiting for the other one to appear. I could not afford to remain hidden any longer: I stepped down from the Niche and walked towards the Other.

He glanced up and scowled as I approached. He did not pause in pumping up his boat. About two metres to his left was the grey bag, now empty, and beside it, resting on the Pavement, was the silver Gun.

'Where the Hell have you been?' he said in a voice of displeasure and anger. 'Why weren't you there on Tuesday? I looked for you everywhere. I can't remember if you said that ten rooms will be flooded or a hundred.' His foot on the pump was slowing; the inflatable boat was almost full of Air and his foot was meeting with more resistance. 'I've had to change my plans. It's a pain, but there it is. Raphael is coming here and, like it or not, we're going to finish this. So no nonsense from you, all right? Because I swear, Piranesi, I've just about had enough from everyone.'

'*I visited him in mid-November,*' I said. '*It was just after four, a cold blue twilight.*'

He stopped pumping. The boat was now a plump shape with a taut, rounded skin. 'We attach the seats next,' he said. 'They're those black things over there. Pass them to me, will you?' He pointed to the two contraptions whose purpose I had not divined. 'When the room floods, you and I will get into this kayak. If Raphael tries to get into it with us, or to hang on to it, use your paddle to strike at her hands and head.'

'*The afternoon had been stormy,*' I said, '*and the lights of the cars were pixelated by rain; the pavements collaged with wet black leaves.*'

He was fiddling with the valves where the Air had gone in. 'What?' he asked, irritably. 'What are you talking about? Can you hurry up and pass me those seats? We need to get a move on. She'll be here any moment now.'

'*When I got to his house I heard music playing,*' I said. '*A requiem. I waited for him to answer the door to an accompaniment of Berlioz.*'

'Berlioz?' He stopped what he was doing, straightened and looked at me properly for the first time. He frowned. 'I don't ... Berlioz?'

I said: '*The door opened. "Dr Ketterley?" I said.*'

He froze at the sound of his own name. His eyes widened. 'What are you talking about?' he asked again in a voice made hoarse with fear.

'Battersea,' I said. 'You asked me once if I remembered Battersea. And now I do.'

Boom! ... ... *Boom!* ... ... The Tide from the Twenty-Second Vestibule was growing stronger; it was hitting the Walls of the Second and Third South-Western Halls with more force.

'You saw her message,' he said.

'Yes,' I said.

A thin Ripple of Water raced across the Pavement and hit my feet. It was followed immediately by another one.

He laughed suddenly, an odd sound: hysteria masquerading as relief. 'No, no!' he said. 'You don't get me that easily. Those aren't your words. They're someone else's. You don't really remember. Raphael put you up to this. Really, Matthew, how stupid do you think I am?'

He dived suddenly to the right, towards the Gun that was lying on the Pavement. But I had chosen my position with care and I was nearer to it than he was. I gave it a good, sharp kick with my foot. It skittered across the marble Pavement and came to rest by the Northern Wall about fifteen metres away. More Ripples – deeper now – were coursing past our feet. They flowed after the Gun, as if we were all playing a game with the Gun and they intended to catch it.

'What … ? What are you going to do?' asked the Other.

'Where is 16?' I asked.

He opened his mouth to say something, but at that moment a voice was heard. 'Ketterley!' it cried. A woman's voice. 16 was here!

From the sound I judged that she was hidden in one of the Southern Doors. The Other, who is not accustomed to the way in which the echoes reverberate in the Halls, looked around him in a confused manner.

'Ketterley,' she shouted again. 'I've come for Matthew Rose Sorensen.'

He grabbed me by my right arm. 'He's here!' he shouted. 'I have him! Come and get him.'

The Booming of the Tides was growing louder. The whole Hall reverberated with the Force of it. Water was flowing freely in through all the Southern Doors.

'Take care!' I shouted. 'He means you harm. He has a Gun!'

A small, slight figure stepped out of the Door that leads to the First Southern Hall. She wore jeans and a green jumper. Her dark hair was pulled back into a ponytail.

The Other let go of me with his right hand (though he still had hold of me by his left). Then he made a fist of his right hand and he swung his arm and body back, intending to get some momentum to hit me; but I swung with him, overbalancing him. He half-fell to the Floor. I pulled free from him and began to run towards 16.

As I ran, I shouted: 'A Flood is coming! We must climb!'

I do not know how much of my words she heard, but she understood the urgency in my voice. I seized her hand. Together we ran towards the Eastern Wall.

The Statues of the Horned Giants were in front of us on either side of the Eastern Door, but we could not climb them; their bodies emerged from the Wall two metres above the Floor and there were no hand- or footholds until that point. Next to the Giant on the left was the Statue of a Father seated with his little Son in his Arms; the Father was plucking a thorn from his Son's Foot. I climbed into their Niche and then onto their Plinth. I mounted onto the Father's lap and by holding onto one of the Columns at the side, and using the Arm, Shoulder and Head of the Father as footholds, I climbed onto the Top of the triangular Pediment that surmounted the Niche. 16 tried to follow me, but she was not so tall as me and, I suspect, not accustomed to climbing. She got as far as the Statue's lap but seemed at a loss what to do next. Quickly I climbed down again and lifted her up; with my help, she heaved herself up onto the Pediment.

It was noon. In the Tenth and Twenty-Fourth Vestibules the last two Tides were rising, filling the surrounding Area with tempestuous, raging Waters.

Half a metre above the Pediment was a Deep Cornice or Shelf that ran the whole length of the Hall. We scaled the slope of the Pediment and hoisted ourselves onto the Cornice above. We were now about seven metres above the Floor. 16 was pale and shaking (she clearly did not love climbing), but she had a fierce, determined expression.

The Air was suddenly rent by sharp, cracking sounds – perhaps four of them – one after the other. For one terrifying moment I thought that the Weight and Vibrations of the Waters were causing the Hall to collapse. I looked out into the Hall and I saw that the Other had not yet got into his boat (where he would be safe); instead he had run to the Northern Wall to retrieve his Gun. He was firing at us.

'Get in the boat!' I shouted to him. 'Get in the boat before it is too late!'

He fired again, hitting a Statue above our heads. I felt a sharp pain in my forehead. I cried out. I put my hand up and brought it away covered in blood.

The Other started to wade through the running Waters towards us – presumably with the idea of firing his Gun at us more effectively.

I shouted at him again, something to the effect that the Tides were almost here! – but there was a Great Roar of Waters from every direction and I doubt that he heard me.

If there had not been someone firing a Gun at us, we could have stayed on the Cornice. (Then, if the Waters rose higher than I expected, we could have climbed up again.) But, as matters stood, we were exposed, without protection.

A metre or so below us the Back and Upper Arms of the Horned Giant emerged from the Wall. There was a Space between his Back and the Wall, a sort of marble pocket. I jumped; it was a distance of approximately two metres sideways, one metre down; I managed it with ease. I looked up at 16. Her eyes were wide with apprehension. I held out my arms. She jumped. I caught her.

We were now shielded from the Other's Gun by the Giant's Body. I heaved Myself up his marble Back to look over his Shoulder.

The Other had turned away from us and was trying to reach the boat. But he had left it too late. The Waters were as high as his knees and the contending Waves were dragging at him. As he struggled, he seemed to grow heavier; the boat by contrast grew lighter, freer. It danced on the Waters, spun from one Part of the Hall to another; one moment it was by the Northern Wall, the next it was halfway to the Western Wall. The Other kept changing direction to follow it, but by the time he had taken a few arduous steps, the boat was somewhere else entirely.

Suddenly it was as if the boat remembered the purpose for which it had been brought here; it seemed to make up its mind to save him. It turned and sailed directly towards him. He held out his arms and leant forwards to catch it. It was barely half a metre from his grasp. For an instant I think he had his hand on its bow; then it twirled around and was gone, borne away to the Western End of the Hall.

'Climb! Climb!' I shouted. It was too late to catch the boat, but I thought that if he climbed, he might still save himself. But he could not hear me above the Sound of the Waters pouring into the Hall. He continued to wade desperately, uselessly, after the boat.

There was a Great Rush and a Great Roar in the next Hall; a Weight of Water hit the other side of the Northern Wall. *Boom!!!* And then I was grateful that we had climbed down to the Horned Giant. If we had still been standing on the Cornice, we would have been flung off the Wall. But the Horned Giant held us fast.

Spray as high as the Ceiling exploded through all the Northern Doors. The Spray caught the Sun; it was as if someone had suddenly thrown a hundred barrelfuls of diamonds into the Hall.

Great Waves surged through the Northern Doors. One plucked up the Other and threw him against the Southern Wall. He crashed into the Statues at a point about fifteen metres from the Floor. I imagine that that was when he died.

The Wave drew back; he disappeared into it.

Meanwhile the little inflatable boat whirled about on the Waters, sometimes engulfed by them for a moment or two, but always reappearing immediately. If he could only have reached it, it would have saved him.

Raphael

SECOND ENTRY FOR THE TWENTY-SEVENTH DAY OF THE NINTH MONTH IN THE YEAR THE ALBATROSS CAME TO THE SOUTH-WESTERN HALLS

Waves crashed against the Southern Wall; explosions of white Spray filled the Hall. The Waters covered the Bottom Tier of Statues; the colour of the Waters was a stormy grey and their Depths were black. Several times Waves passed over our heads, but they fell back the next instant. We were drenched, we were numbed, we were blinded, we were deafened; but always we were saved.

Time passed.

The Waves sank down and the Waters became peaceable. They began to drain away into the Staircases and the Lower Halls. The Heads of the Bottom Tier of Statues reappeared above the Surface of the Waters.

In all this time 16 and I had not spoken to each other. The Roar of the Waves would have made it impossible for us to hear each other and in any case, we had been intent on saving ourselves and each other; we had had no thought for anything else. Now we turned and looked at each other.

16 had large dark eyes and an elfin face. Her expression was solemn. She was a little older than me – about forty, I thought. Her hair was black with wet.

'You are Six ... You are Raphael,' I said.

'I'm Sarah Raphael,' she said. 'And you are Matthew Rose Sorensen.'

And you are Matthew Rose Sorensen. This time she framed it as a statement, rather than a question. This was surely premature. It would have been better to keep it as a question. But then again, if she *had* framed it as a question, I would not have known how to answer it.

'Did he know you?' I asked.

'Did who know me?' she said.

'Matthew Rose Sorensen. Did Matthew Rose Sorensen know you? Is that why you came here?'

She paused, taking in what I had just said. Then she said carefully, 'No. You and I have never met.'

'Then why?'

'I'm a police officer,' she said.

'Oh,' I said.

We fell back into silence. We were both still dazed by what had happened. Our eyes were still full of images of the Violent Waters; our ears were still full of their Sounds; our minds were still full of that moment when the Other was flung by the Wave against the Wall of Statues. We had nothing at that moment to say to each other.

Raphael turned her attention to practical matters. She examined the injury to my forehead and said that it was not very deep. She did not think that I had been hit by one of the Other's bullets; more likely I had been grazed by a shard of splintered marble.

The Level of the Waters continued to fall. When they came no higher than the Plinths of the Bottom Tier of Statues, I began to consider how we would get down from the Horned Giant. We could not return the way we had come since that would involve a leap upwards onto the Cornice. I did not think that Raphael could manage it. (Indeed, I was not sure that I could either.)

'I'll go and fetch something to help you climb down,' I told her. 'Don't be anxious. I'll return as quickly as I can.'

I lowered Myself from the Giant's Torso and dropped down. The Waters reached as high as my thighs. I waded to the Third Northern Hall and climbed up the Statues to the places where I keep my belongings. Everything was wet from the Spray, but nothing was drenched. I retrieved my fishing nets, a bottle of

Fresh Water and some dried seaweed. (It is important to keep the body hydrated and nourished.)

I returned to the First Western Hall. The Waters had already dropped some more and only came up as high as my knees. I climbed back up the Horned Giant. I gave Raphael some water and made her eat a little of the dried seaweed (though I do not think she liked it). Then I tied my fishing nets together and fastened them to one of the Giant's Arms. They hung down to a point about half a metre above the Pavement. I showed Raphael how to use the fishing nets to climb down.

We waded to the First Vestibule and ascended the Great Staircase so that we were out of the reach of the Waters. We sat down. Our clothes were plastered to our bodies with wet. My hair – which is dark and curly – was as full of droplets as a Cloud. I rained every time I moved.

The birds found us there. Many different kinds – herring gulls, rooks, blackbirds and sparrows – gathered on the Statues and Banisters and chattered at me in their different voices.

'It'll be gone soon,' I told them. 'Don't worry.'

'What?' asked Raphael, startled. 'I don't understand.'

'I was talking to the birds,' I said. 'They're alarmed by the great quantities of Water that are everywhere. I'm telling them that it'll soon be gone.'

'Oh!' She said. 'Do you ... Do you do talk to the birds often?'

'Yes,' I said. 'But there's no need to look surprised. You talked to the birds yourself. In the Sixth North-Western Hall. I heard you.'

She looked even more surprised at that. 'What did I say?' she asked.

'You told them to piss off. You were writing a message to me and they were being a nuisance, flying in your face and over your writing, trying to find out what you were doing.'

She thought a moment. 'Was that the message that you wiped out?' she asked.

'Yes.'

'Why did you do that?'

'Because the Oth ... Because Dr Ketterley told me you were my enemy and that reading what you had written would make me go mad. So I erased the message. But at the same time, I wanted to read it, so I didn't erase all of it. I wasn't being very logical.'

'He made things very hard for you.'

'Yes. I suppose he did.'

There was a silence.

'We're both soaking wet and cold,' said Raphael. 'Perhaps we should go?'

'Go where?' I said.

'Home,' said Raphael. 'I mean we can go to my house and get dry. And then I can take you home.'

'I am home,' I said.

Raphael looked around at the sombre grey Waters lapping the Walls and the dripping Statues. She didn't say anything.

'It's usually a lot drier than this,' I said quickly in case she was thinking that my Home was inhospitable and damp.

But that wasn't what she was thinking.

'There's something I have to tell you,' she said. 'I don't know if you remember this, but you have a mum and a dad. And two sisters. And friends.' She gazed at me intently. 'Do you remember?'

I shook my head.

'They've been looking for you,' she said. 'But they didn't know the right place to look. They've been worried about you. They've been … ' She looked away again to find the right words to express her thought. 'They've felt pain because they didn't know where you were,' she said.

I considered this. 'I'm sorry that Matthew Rose Sorensen's mum and dad and sisters and friends feel pain,' I said. 'But I don't really see what it has to do with me.'

'You don't think of yourself as Matthew Rose Sorensen?'

'No,' I said.

'But you have his face,' she said.

'Yes.'

'And his hands.'

'Yes.'

'And his feet and his body.'

'All that is true. But I haven't got his mind and I haven't got his memories. I don't mean that he's not here. He is here.' I touched my breast. 'But I think he's asleep. He's fine. You mustn't worry about him.'

She nodded. She was not a contentious person as the Other had been; she did not argue and contradict everything I said. I liked that about her. 'Who are you?' she asked. 'If you're not him.'

'I am the Beloved Child of the House,' I said.

'The house? What is the house?'

Such a strange question! I spread my arms to indicate the First Vestibule, the Halls beyond the First Vestibule, Everything. 'This is the House. Look!'

'Oh. I see.'

We were silent a moment.

Then Raphael said, 'I need to ask you something. Would you be prepared to come with me to Matthew Rose Sorensen's parents and sisters – to let them see his face again? It would help them a lot to know he is alive. Even if you had to go away again – I mean even if you had to return here, it would help them. What do you think about that?'

'I can't do it now,' I said.

'OK.'

'I have to consider the needs of the Biscuit-Box Man – and the Folded-Up Child – and the People of the Alcove. They only have me to take care of them. They are in unfamiliar surroundings and may feel disconcerted. I have to return them to their appointed places.'

'There are other people here?' asked Raphael, in surprise.

'Yes.'

'How many?'

'Thirteen. The ones I have just said and also the Concealed Person. But the Concealed Person resides in one of the Upper Halls and has not been affected by the Flood so there was no need to move him or her.'

'Thirteen people!' Raphael's dark eyes were wide with astonishment. 'My God! Are they all right?'

'Yes,' I said. 'They're fine. I take good care of them.'

'But who are they? Can you take me to them? Is Stanley Ovenden here? What about Sylvia D'Agostino? Maurizio Giussani?'

'Oh, it is highly probable that one of them is Stanley Ovenden. Certainly the Proph ... Certainly Laurence Arne-Sayles thought so. Another may be Sylvia D'Agostino and another Maurizio Giussani. Unfortunately, I have no idea which is which.'

'What do you mean? Have they forgotten who they are? What do they say?'

'Oh, they don't say much really. They're all dead.'

'Dead!'

'Yes.'

'Oh!' Raphael took a moment to process this. 'Were they dead when you arrived?' she asked.

'I ... ' I paused. It was an interesting question. I hadn't considered it before. 'I think so,' I said. 'I think they've all been dead a long time, but as I don't remember arriving, I can't be certain. Arriving was something that happened to Matthew Rose Sorensen, not to me.'

'Yes, I suppose that's right. But what do you mean, you take care of them?'

'I make sure they are in good order. As complete and tidy as they can be. I bring them offerings of food and drink and water lilies. And I talk to them. Don't you have Dead of your own in your Halls?'

'I do. Yes.'

'Don't you take them offerings? Don't you talk to them?'

Before Raphael could answer this another thought struck me. 'I said there are thirteen Dead, but that is incorrect. Dr

Ketterley has joined their number. I must find his body and make him ready to lie with the others.' I clapped my hands together. 'So, as you see, I have a great many tasks to perform and cannot at the moment think about leaving these Halls.'

Raphael nodded slowly. 'That's OK,' she said. 'There's plenty of time.' She put out her hand and rather awkwardly – but also gently – put her hand on my shoulder.

Instantly, and to my huge embarrassment, I started crying. Great creaking sobs rose up in my chest and tears sprouted from my eyes. I did not think that it was me who was crying; it was Matthew Rose Sorensen crying through my eyes. It lasted for a long time until it tailed off into braying, hiccupping gulps for Air.

Raphael still had her hand on my shoulder. She looked away tactfully while I wiped my eyes and my nose with the back of my hand.

'You will come back?' I said. 'Even though I don't go with you now, you will come back?'

'I'll come back tomorrow,' she said. 'It'll be rather late in the evening. Will that be OK? How will we find each other?'

'I'll wait for you here,' I said. 'It doesn't matter how late it is. I'll wait until you come.'

'And you'll think about what I said? About coming to see your ... to see Matthew Rose Sorensen's parents and sisters?'

'Yes,' I said. 'I'll think about it.'

Raphael left, disappearing into the Shadowy Space between the two Minotaurs in the South-Eastern Corner of the Vestibule.

My watch had stopped, but I estimated it to be early evening. I was alone, exhausted, hungry and wet. I waded back to the Third Northern Hall. The Water was still a half-metre deep. I climbed up and examined the dry seaweed that I use to build fires. Unfortunately it had been thoroughly wetted by the Great Waves. I could not make a fire. I could not cook anything.

I fetched my sleeping bag – also damp – and took it to the First Vestibule. I lay down on a Dry, High Step of the Great Staircase.

My last thought before I fell asleep was: *He is dead. My only friend. My only enemy.*

I comfort Dr Ketterley

ENTRY FOR THE TWENTY-EIGHTH DAY OF THE NINTH MONTH IN THE YEAR THE ALBATROSS CAME TO THE SOUTH-WESTERN HALLS

I found Dr Ketterley's body in an Angle of the Staircase in the Eighth Vestibule. He had been battered against the Walls and the Statues. His clothes were in rags. I disentangled him from the Balustrade and laid him out straight and composed his limbs. I took his poor, broken head into my lap and cradled it.

'Your good looks are gone,' I told him. 'But you mustn't worry about it. This unsightly condition is only temporary. Don't be sad. Don't fear. I will place you somewhere where the fish and the birds can strip away all this broken flesh. It will soon be gone. Then you will be a handsome skull and handsome bones. I will put you in good order and you can rest in the Sunlight and the Starlight. The Statues will look down on you with Blessing. I am sorry that I was angry with you. Forgive me.'

I did not find the Gun – the Tides must have taken it deep within themselves; but later that morning I found Dr Ketterley's boat, still idling on the Waters in the First Western Hall which were now no more than ankle-deep. It was quite unharmed.

'I wish that you had saved him,' I told it.

I did not feel that it responded in any way. It seemed drowsy, dozing, only half alive. Without the Rushing Waters to animate it, it was no longer the devil that had danced on the Waves, first mocking Dr Ketterley and then abandoning him.

I have been thinking about what Raphael said about Matthew Rose Sorensen's mum and his dad and his sisters and his friends. Perhaps I should send them a message explaining that Matthew Rose Sorensen now lives inside me, that he is unconscious but perfectly safe, and that I am a strong and resourceful person who will care for him assiduously, exactly as I care for any others of the Dead.

I shall ask Raphael what she thinks of this idea.

As the Shadows fell in the First Vestibule Raphael returned

SECOND ENTRY FOR THE TWENTY-EIGHTH DAY OF THE NINTH MONTH IN THE YEAR THE ALBATROSS CAME TO THE SOUTH-WESTERN HALLS

As the Shadows fell in the First Vestibule Raphael returned. We sat on a Step of the Great Staircase as before. Raphael had a shining little device like the one that the Other had. She tapped it and it brought forth a shaft of white-yellow Light to illuminate the Statues and our faces.

I told Raphael my plan to write to Matthew Rose Sorensen's mum and dad and two sisters and friends, but for some reason she did not think this was a good idea.

'What should I call you?' she asked.

'Call me?' I said.

'As a name. If you're not Matthew Rose Sorensen, then what should I call you?'

'Oh, I see. I suppose you could call me Pir ... ' I stopped. 'Dr Ketterley used to call me Piranesi,' I said. 'He said it was a name to do with labyrinths, but I think perhaps it was meant to mock me.'

'Probably,' agreed Raphael. 'He was that sort of guy.' There was a little silence and then she said, 'Would you like to know how I found you?'

'Very much,' I said.

'There was a woman. I don't suppose you remember her. Her name was Angharad Scott. She wrote a book about Laurence Arne-Sayles. Six years ago, you contacted her. You told her that you were also thinking of writing a book about Arne-Sayles and the two of you had a long conversation. Then she never heard from you again. In May of this year she called the college in London where you used to work because she wanted to know what had happened about the book – whether you were still writing it. The people at the college told her that you were missing; that you'd been missing pretty much the entire time since she'd first spoken to you. That rang all sorts of warning bells for Mrs Scott because she knew about the people who had disappeared around Arne-Sayles. You were the fourth – the fifth if you count Jimmy Ritter. So she contacted us. It was the first time that we – I mean the police – knew that there was any connection between you and Arne-Sayles. When we talked to the people who remained of Arne-Sayles's circle – Bannerman, Hughes, Ketterley and Arne-Sayles himself – it was obvious something was going on. Tali Hughes kept crying and saying she was sorry. Arne-Sayles was thrilled by the attention and Ketterley couldn't open his mouth without lying.' She paused. 'Do you understand any of what I'm saying?'

'A little,' I said. 'Matthew Rose Sorensen wrote about all these people. I know that they are connected to the Proph ... to Laurence Arne-Sayles. Did he tell you where I was? He said that he would.'

'Who?'

'Laurence Arne-Sayles.'

Raphael took a moment to process this. 'You spoke to him?' she asked in a tone of incredulity.

'Yes.'

'He *came* here?'

'Yes.'

'When?'

'About two months ago.'

'And he didn't offer to help you? He didn't offer to take you out of here?'

'No. But to be fair, if he had offered I wouldn't have wanted to go. In fact, I'm still not sure that I want to go.'

A pale owl glided out of the First Eastern Hall into the First Vestibule. It settled on a Statue high up on the Southern Wall where it gleamed whitely in the Dimness. I have seen owls portrayed in marble. Many Statues incorporate them. But I had never seen their living counterpart until now. Its appearance was, I felt sure, connected with the coming of Raphael and the departure of Dr Ketterley; it was as though a principle of Death had been replaced with a principle of Life. Things, I thought, were speeding up.

Raphael had not perceived the owl. She said, 'You're right. Arne-Sayles told us the truth straightaway. He said you were in the labyrinth. But of course ... Well, we thought he was just trying to wind us up. Which was right. He *was* just trying to wind us up. My colleagues put up with it for a while, but they gave up on him eventually. I had a different idea. I thought: he likes talking. Just let him. Eventually he'll say something useful.'

She tapped her shining little device. It spoke with Laurence Arne-Sayles's haughty, drawling voice: *'You think that all my talk about other worlds is irrelevant. But it isn't. It's absolutely key. Matthew Rose Sorensen attempted to enter another world. If he hadn't done that, he wouldn't have "disappeared" as you call it.'*

Raphael's voice answered him: *'Something about the attempt caused him to disappear?'*

'Yes.' Laurence Arne-Sayles again.

'Something happened to him during this ... this ritual, whatever it was? Why? Where do these rituals take place?'

'You mean do we perform them on the edge of a precipice and he just fell off? No, nothing like that. Besides, it needn't necessarily have been a ritual. I never use them myself.'

'But why would he do that?' asked Raphael. *'Why would he perform the ritual or do whatever it is? There's nothing in what he wrote to suggest he believed your theories. Quite the reverse in fact.'*

'*Oh,* belief,' said Arne-Sayles, laying a deep, sarcastic emphasis on the word. '*Why do people always think it's a question of belief? It's not. People can "believe" whatever they want. I really couldn't care less.*'

'*Yes, but if he didn't believe, why would he even try?*'

'*Because he had half a brain and he recognised that mine was one of the great intellects of the twentieth century — perhaps the greatest of all. And he wanted to understand me. So he made the attempt to reach another world, not because he thought the other world existed, but because he thought the attempt itself would grant him insight into my thinking. Into me. And now you are going to do the same.*'

'*Me?*' Raphael sounded startled.

'*Yes. And you are going to do it for the exact same reason that Rose Sorensen did it. He wanted to understand my thinking. You want to understand his. Adjust your perceptions in the way I am about to describe to you. Perform the actions that I will outline for you and then you will know.*'

'*What will I know, Laurence?*'

'*You'll know what happened to Matthew Rose Sorensen.*'

'*It's that simple?*'

'*Oh, yes. It's that simple.*'

Raphael tapped the device; the voices fell silent.

'I didn't think that was a bad idea,' she said, 'to try and understand what you'd been thinking at the point you dis appeared. Arne-Sayles described what to do, how to go back to a pre-rational mode of thought. He said that when I'd done that, I'd see paths all around me and he told me which one to choose. I thought he meant metaphorical paths. It was a bit of a shock when it turned out he didn't.'

'Yes,' I said. 'Matthew Rose Sorensen was shocked when he first arrived. Shocked and frightened. And then he fell asleep and I was born. Later I found entries in my Journal that frightened me. I thought that I must have been mad when I wrote them. But now I understand that Matthew Rose Sorensen wrote them and he was describing a different World.'

'Yes.'

'And the Other World has different things in it. Words such as "Manchester" and "police station" have no meaning here. Because those things do not exist. Words such as "river" and "mountain" do have meaning but only because those things are depicted in the Statues. I suppose that these things must exist in the Older World. In this World the Statues depict things that exist in the Older World.'

'Yes,' said Raphael. 'Here you can only see a representation of a river or a mountain, but in our world – the other world – you can see the actual river and the actual mountain.'

This annoyed me. 'I do not see why you say I can *only* see a representation in this World,' I said with some sharpness. 'The word "only" suggests a relationship of inferiority. You make it sound as if the Statue was somehow inferior to the thing itself. I do not see that that is the case at all. I would argue that the Statue is superior to the thing itself, the Statue being perfect, eternal and not subject to decay.'

'Sorry,' said Raphael. 'I didn't mean to disparage your world.'

There was a silence.

'What is the Other World like?' I asked.

Raphael looked as if she did not know quite how to answer this question. 'There are more people,' she said at last.

'A lot more?' I asked.

'Yes.'

'As many as seventy?' I asked, deliberately choosing a high, rather improbable number.

'Yes,' she said. Then she smiled.

'Why do you smile?' I asked.

'It's the way you raise your eyebrow at me. That dubious, rather imperious look. Do you know who you look like when you do that?'

'No. Who?'

'You look like Matthew Rose Sorensen. Like photos of him that I've seen.'

'How do you know that there are more than seventy people?' I asked. 'Have you counted them yourself?'

'No, but I'm fairly sure,' she said. 'It's not always a pleasant world, the other world. There's a lot of sadness.' She paused. 'A lot of sadness,' she said again. 'It's not like here.' She sighed. 'I need you to understand something. Whether you come back with me or not, it's up to you. Ketterley tricked you. He kept you here with lies and deceit. I don't want to trick you. You must only come if you want to.'

'And if I stay here will you come back and visit me?' I said.

'Of course,' she said.

Other people

ENTRY FOR THE TWENTY-NINTH DAY OF THE NINTH MONTH IN THE YEAR THE ALBATROSS CAME TO THE SOUTH-WESTERN HALLS

For as long as I can remember I have wanted to show the House to someone. I used to imagine that the Sixteenth Person was at my side and that I would say to him such things as:

Now we enter the First Northern Hall. Observe the many beautiful Statues. On your right you will see the Statue of an Old Man holding the Model of a Ship, on your left is the Statue of a Winged Horse and its Colt.

I imagined us visiting the Drowned Halls together:

Now we descend through this Gash in the Floor; we climb down the fallen Masonry and enter the Hall below. Place your feet where I place mine and you will have no difficulty keeping your balance. The immense Statues that are a feature of these Halls provide us with safe places to sit. Observe the dark, still Waters. We may gather water lilies here and present them to the Dead ...

Today all my imaginings came true. The Sixteenth Person and I walked together through the House and I showed her many things.

She arrived in the First Vestibule early in the morning.

'Will you do something for me?' she asked.

'Of course,' I said. 'Anything.'

'Show me the labyrinth.'

'Gladly. What would you like to see?'

'I don't know,' she said. 'Whatever you want to show me. Whatever's most beautiful.'

Of course, what I really wanted to show her was *everything*, but that was impossible. My first thought was the Drowned Halls, but I remembered that Raphael did not love climbing, so I decided on the Coral Halls, a long succession of Halls extending south and west from the Thirty-Eighth Southern Hall.

We walked through the Southern Halls. Raphael looked relaxed and happy. (I was happy too.) With every step Raphael was looking around with pleasure and admiration.

She said, 'It's such an astonishing place. A perfect place. I saw some of it while I was looking for you, but I kept having to stop at the doors to write out the directions back to the minotaur room. It got very time-consuming and frustrating and of course I didn't dare go too far in case I made a mistake.'

'You wouldn't have made a mistake,' I assured her. 'Your directions were excellent.'

'How long did it take you to learn it? The way through the labyrinth?' she asked.

I opened my mouth to say loudly and boastfully that I have always known it, that it is part of me, that the House and I could not be separated. But I realised, before I even spoke the words, that it was not true. I remembered that I used to mark the Doorways with chalk in exactly the same way that Raphael did and I remembered that I used to be afraid of getting lost. I shook my head. 'I don't know,' I said. 'I can't remember.'

'Is it all right to take photos?' She held up her shining device. 'Or is that not . . . ? I don't know, is that disrespectful in some way?'

'Of course you may take photos,' I said. 'I took photographs sometimes for the Oth . . . for Dr Ketterley.'

But I was pleased that she had asked the question. It showed that she regarded the House as I did, as something deserving of respect. (Dr Ketterley never learnt this. He seemed incapable of it somehow.)

In the Tenth Southern Hall I made a detour to the Fourteenth South-Western Hall to show Raphael the People of the Alcove.

There are (as I have explained before) ten of them and the skeleton of a monkey.

Raphael regarded them gravely. She gently rested her hand on one of the bones – the tibia of one of the males. It was a gesture conveying comfort and reassurance. *Don't be afraid. You are safe. I am here.*

'We don't know who they are,' she said. 'Poor things.'

'They are the People of the Alcove,' I said.

'Arne-Sayles probably murdered at least one of them. Perhaps he murdered all of them.'

These were solemn words. Before I could decide how I felt about them she turned to me and said with great intensity, 'I'm sorry. I'm really, really sorry.'

I was astonished, even a little alarmed. No one has ever been as kind to me as Raphael; no one has ever done more for me. That she should apologise seemed to me inappropriate. 'No ... No ... ' I murmured and I put up my hands to fend off her words.

But she went on with a bleak, angry look on her face. 'He'll never be punished for what he did to you. Or for what he did to them. I've gone over it and over it in my mind and there's nothing I can do. Nothing he can be charged with. Not without a lot of explanation that literally no one will want to believe.' She sighed deeply. 'I said that this is a perfect world. But it's not. There are crimes here, just like everywhere else.'

A wave of sadness and helplessness washed over me. I wanted to say that the People of the Alcove had not been murdered by Arne-Sayles (though I have no evidence to support that assertion and the probability is that at least one of them was).

Mostly I wanted Raphael to come away from them so that I could stop thinking of them the way she thought of them – as murdered – and go back to thinking of them the way I always had before – as good, and noble, and peaceful.

We continued on our way, stopping often to admire a particularly striking Statue. Our hearts grew lighter again and when we reached the Coral Halls, we refreshed ourselves with looking at their wonders.

Though the Coral Halls are dry now, it appears that at one time they were flooded with Sea Water for a long period. Coral has grown there, changing the Statues in strange and unexpected ways. One may see, for example, a Woman crowned with coral, her Hands transformed into stars or flowers. There are Figures horned with coral, or crucified on coral branches, or stuck through with coral arrows. There is a Lion enmeshed in a cage of coral and a Man holding a Little Box. The coral has grown so profusely over his Left Side that half of him appears to be engulfed in red- and rose-coloured flames, while the other half is not.

Late in the afternoon we returned to the First Vestibule. Just before we parted Raphael said, 'I love the quiet here. No people!' She said the last part as if it were the greatest advantage of all.

'Don't you like the people in your own Halls?' I asked, puzzled.

'I like them,' she said, with no very great enthusiasm. 'Mostly I like them. Some of them. I don't always get them. They don't always get me.'

After she had gone, I thought about what she had said. I cannot imagine not wanting to be with people. (Though it is true that Dr Ketterley was sometimes annoying.) I remembered how Raphael had wondered which of the People of the Alcove had been murdered and how the simple fact of her posing the question had made the whole World seem a darker, sadder Place.

Perhaps that is what it is like being with other people. Perhaps even people you like and admire immensely can make you see the World in ways you would rather not. Perhaps that is what Raphael means.

Strange emotions

ENTRY FOR THE THIRTIETH DAY OF THE NINTH MONTH IN THE YEAR THE ALBATROSS CAME TO THE SOUTH-WESTERN HALLS

I once wrote in my Journal:

> *It is my belief that the World (or, if you will, the House, since the two are for all practical purposes identical) wishes an Inhabitant for Itself to be a witness to its Beauty and the recipient of its Mercies.*

If I leave, then the House will have no Inhabitant and how will I bear the thought of it Empty?

Yet the simple fact is that if I remain in these Halls I will be alone. In one sense I suppose I will be no more alone than before. Raphael has promised to visit me, just as the Other visited me before. And Raphael really is my friend – whereas the Other's feelings towards me were mixed, to say the least. Whenever the Other left me he went back to his own World, but I did not know that at the time; I thought that he was simply in another Part of the House. Believing that there was someone else here made me less lonely. Now, when Raphael returns to the Other World, I will know that I am alone.

And so for this reason I have decided to go with Raphael.

I have returned all of the Dead to their allotted places. Today I walked through the Halls as I have done a thousand times before. I visited all my most beloved Statues and as I gazed on each one, I thought: *Perhaps this will be the last time I look on your Face. Goodbye! Goodbye!*

I leave

ENTRY FOR THE FIRST DAY OF THE TENTH MONTH IN THE YEAR THE ALBATROSS CAME TO THE SOUTH-WESTERN HALLS

This morning I fetched the small cardboard box with the word AQUARIUM and the picture of an octopus on it. It is the box that originally contained the shoes Dr Ketterley gave me. When Dr Ketterley told me to hide Myself from 16, I took the ornaments out of my hair and placed them in the box. But now, wanting to look my best when I enter the New World, I spent two or three hours putting them back in, all the pretty things that I have found or made: seashells, coral beads, pearls, tiny pebbles and interesting fishbones.

When Raphael arrived, she seemed rather astonished at my pleasant appearance.

I took my messenger bag with all my Journals and my favourite pens and we walked towards the two Minotaurs in the South-Eastern Corner. The shadows between them shimmered slightly. The shadows suggested the shape of a corridor or alleyway with dim walls and, at the end of it, lights, flashes of moving colour that my eye could not interpret.

I took one last look at the Eternal House. I shivered. Raphael took my hand. Then, together, we walked into the corridor.

PART 7

MATTHEW ROSE SORENSEN

Valentine Ketterley has disappeared

Valentine Ketterley, psychologist and anthropologist, has disappeared. The police have made inquiries and discovered that before his disappearance he made some unusual purchases: a gun, an inflatable kayak and a life-jacket – purchases that his friends all agree were completely out of character: he had never shown any inclination to be waterborne before.

None of these items has been found in his house or office.

The police think that possibly he used the inflatable kayak to travel to a remote spot and then used the gun to kill himself; but there is one officer, a man called Jamie Askill, who has a different idea. He believes that the sudden and unexpected disappearance of Dr Ketterley must be linked in some way to the sudden and unexpected reappearance of Matthew Rose Sorensen. Askill's theory is that Ketterley imprisoned Rose Sorensen somewhere, in the same way that Ketterley's one-time supervisor and tutor, Laurence Arne-Sayles, imprisoned James Ritter years before. Ketterley's motive, thinks Askill, was the same as Arne-Sayles's: to manufacture evidence of Arne-Sayles's Theory of Other Worlds. Ketterley became alarmed when the police uncovered the link between himself and Rose Sorensen. Faced with the exposure of his crimes, Ketterley let Rose Sorensen go and then killed himself.

Askill's theory has the advantage of accounting for the reappearance of Matthew Rose Sorensen at the same time – give or take a day or two – that Ketterley disappeared, which is otherwise an odd coincidence. Where the theory falls down is that neither Arne-Sayles nor Ketterley ever used the disappearances as evidence of anything. In fact, for many years Ketterley had been loud in his denunciation of Arne-Sayles.

Undeterred, Askill has questioned me twice. He is a young man with a pleasant, good-natured face, little brown curls all over his head and an intelligent expression. He wears a dark blue suit and a grey shirt and speaks with a Yorkshire accent.

'Did you know Valentine Ketterley?' he asks.

'Yes,' I say. 'I visited him in mid-November 2012.'

He looks pleased with this answer. 'That's just before you disappeared,' he points out.

'Yes,' I say.

'And where were you?' he asks. 'While you were gone?'

'I was in a house with many rooms. The sea sweeps through the house. Sometimes it swept over me, but always I was saved.'

Askill pauses and frowns. 'That's not ... You're not ... ' he begins. He thinks for a moment. 'What I mean is that you've had problems. A breakdown of sorts. At least, that's what I've been told. Are you getting treatment for that?'

'My family have arranged for me to see a psychotherapist. To which I have no objection. But I have refused medication and so far, no one has insisted.'

'Well, I hope it helps,' he says, kindly.

'Thank you.'

'What I'm trying to get at,' he says, 'is whether Dr Ketterley persuaded you to go anywhere. Whether he kept you anywhere against your will. Whether you were free to come and go.'

'Yes. I was free. I came and went. I did not remain in one place. I walked for hundreds, perhaps thousands, of kilometres.'

'Oh … Oh, OK. And Dr Ketterley wasn't with you when you walked?'

'No.'

'Was anyone with you?'

'No, I was quite alone.'

'Oh. Oh, well.' Jamie Askill is slightly disappointed. I am disappointed too, in a way: disappointed that I have disappointed him. 'Well,' he says. 'I don't want to take up too much of your time. I know you've already talked to DS Raphael.'

'Yes.'

'She's amazing, isn't she? Raphael?'

'Yes.'

'I'm not surprised that she found you. I mean if anyone was going to find you, it was probably always going to be her.' He pauses. 'Of course, she can be a little … I mean she doesn't really … ' He fishes in the air with his fingers to catch at the elusive words. 'I mean she's not necessarily the easiest person in the world to work with. And time management? Definitely not her thing. But honestly, we all think the world of her.'

'It is right to think the world of Raphael,' I tell him. 'She is an extraordinary person.'

'Exactly. Did anyone ever tell you about Pinny Wheeler?'

'No,' I say. 'Who or what is Pinny Wheeler?'

'A guy in some city in the Midlands – where Raphael started out. He was an upset sort of person, a troubled person, the sort of person that ends up having a lot to do with us.'

'That's not good.'

'No, it's not. There was this one time something happened to set him off and he climbed up inside the cathedral tower. He got onto a sort of gallery and was shouting abuse at the people inside the cathedral. He had some bales of old, dirty newspaper that he used to take everywhere, and he started setting it on fire and throwing it down onto people.'

'How terrible.'

'I know. Frightening, isn't it? When we – I mean the police – got there, it was evening – all dim and dark with flaming sheets of newspaper floating about and people dashing everywhere with fire extinguishers and buckets of sand. Raphael and another guy tried to get to Pinny Wheeller, but when they were in the stairwell – which was a really tight, confined space – Pinny threw a load more burning newspaper down and some of it wrapped itself around the other guy's face. So he had to go back.'

'But Raphael did not go back,' I say, with great certainty.

'No, she didn't. Technically speaking she probably should have, but she didn't. When she came out onto the gallery her hair was on fire. But, you know, she's Raphael. I doubt she even noticed. The people down below had to shout at her to put the fire out. She sat down with Pinny Wheeller and she got him to stop throwing flaming newspaper everywhere and she got him to come down. Pretty brave, don't you think?'

'Braver than you think. She doesn't like heights.'

'She doesn't?'

'They make her uncomfortable.'

'That wouldn't stop her,' he says.

'No.'

'Thank God, she didn't have to do any of that with you. I mean she didn't have to walk through fire or whatever. She just went to the seaside. That's what I heard anyway – that she found you at the seaside.'

'Yes. I was at the side of the sea.'

'A lot of missing people turn up at seaside places,' he muses. 'It's the sea, I suppose. It has a soothing effect.'

'It certainly did on me,' I say.

He smiles cheerfully at me. 'Excellent,' he says.

Matthew Rose Sorensen has reappeared
ENTRY FOR 27 NOVEMBER 2018

Matthew Rose Sorensen's mother and father and sisters and friends all ask me where I have been.

I tell them what I told Jamie Askill: that I was in a house with many rooms; that the sea sweeps through the house; and that sometimes it swept over me, but always I was saved.

Matthew Rose Sorensen's mother and father and sisters and friends tell each other that this is a description of a mental breakdown seen from the inside; an explanation they find reasonable, perhaps even reassuring. They have Matthew Rose Sorensen back – or so they believe. A man with his face and voice and gestures moves about the world, and that is enough for them.

I no longer look like Piranesi. There are no coral beads or fishbones in my hair. My hair is clean and cut and styled. I am clean-shaven. I wear the clothes that were brought to me out of the storage in which Matthew Rose Sorensen's sisters had placed them. Rose Sorensen had a great number of clothes, all meticulously cared for. He had more than a dozen suits (which I find surprising considering that his income was not large). This love of clothes was something he shared with Piranesi. Piranesi frequently wrote about Dr Ketterley's clothes in his journal and lamented the contrast with his own ragged garments. This, I suppose, is where I differ from both of them – from Matthew Rose Sorensen and Piranesi; I find I do not care greatly about clothes.

Many other things were delivered to me out of storage, the most important being Matthew Rose Sorensen's missing journals. They cover the period from June 2000 (when he was an undergraduate) until December 2011. As for the rest of his possessions, I am getting rid of most of them. Piranesi cannot bear to have so many possessions. *I do not need this!* is his constant refrain.

Piranesi is always with me, but of Rose Sorensen I have only hints and shadows. I piece him together out of the objects he has left behind, from what is said about him by other people and, of course, from his journals. Without the journals I would be all at sea.

I remember how this world works – more or less. I remember what Manchester is and what the police are and how to use a smartphone. I can pay for things with money – though I still find the process strange and artificial. Piranesi has a strong dislike of money. Piranesi wants to say: *But I need the thing you have, so why don't you just give it to me? And then when I have something you need, I will just give it to you. This would be a simpler system and much better!*

But I, who am not Piranesi – or at least not only him – realise that this probably wouldn't go down too well.

I have decided to write a book about Laurence Arne-Sayles. It is something that Matthew Rose Sorensen wanted to do and something that I want to do. After all, who knows Arne-Sayles's work better than me?

Raphael has shown me what Laurence Arne-Sayles taught her: how to find the path to the labyrinth and how to find the path out again. I can come and go as I please. Last week I took a train to Manchester. I took a bus to Miles Platting. I walked through a bleak autumn landscape to a flat in a tower block. The door was answered by a thin, ravaged-looking man who smelt strongly of cigarettes.

'Are you James Ritter?' I asked.

He agreed that he was.

'I've come to take you back,' I said.

I led him through the shadowy corridor and when the noble minotaurs of the first vestibule rose up around us, he started to cry, not for fear, but for happiness. He went immediately and sat under the great marble sweep of the staircase; the place where he used to sleep. He closed his eyes and listened to the sounds of the tides. When it was time to leave, he begged me to let him stay, but I refused.

'You don't know how to feed yourself,' I told him. 'You never learnt. You would die here unless I fed you – and I can't

239

take on that responsibility. But I'll bring you back here when-ever you want. And if ever I decide to come back for good, I promise I will bring you with me.'

The body of Valentine Ketterley, magician and scientist

ENTRY FOR 28 NOVEMBER 2018

The body of Valentine Ketterley, magician and scientist, is washed by the tides. I have placed it in one of the lower halls accessed from the eighth vestibule and I have tethered it to the statue of a half-reclining man. The statue's eyes are closed; he is possibly asleep; thick snakes and serpents entwine them-selves heavily with his limbs.

The body is contained in a sack of plastic netting. The mesh of the netting is wide enough for fish to poke their mouths in, and birds their beaks; it is fine enough that none of the small bones will be lost.

I estimate that in six months' time the bones will be white and clean. I will gather them up and take them to the empty niche in the third north-western hall. I will place Valentine Ketterley next to the biscuit-box man. In the middle I will place the long bones tied together with twine. On the right I will place the skull. On the left I will place a box containing all the small bones.

Dr Valentine Ketterley will lie with his colleagues: with Stanley Ovenden, Maurizio Giussani and Sylvia D'Agostino.

Statues again

Piranesi lived among statues: silent presences that brought him comfort and enlightenment.

I thought that in this new (old) world the statues would be irrelevant. I did not imagine that they would continue to help me. But I was wrong. When faced with a person or situation I do not understand, my first impulse is still to look for a statue that will enlighten me.

I think of Dr Ketterley and an image rises up in my mind. It is the memory of a statue that stands in the nineteenth north-western hall. It is the statue of a man kneeling on his plinth; a sword lies at his side, its blade broken in five pieces. Roundabout lie other broken pieces, the remains of a sphere. The man has used his sword to shatter the sphere because he wanted to understand it, but now he finds that he has destroyed both sphere and sword. This puzzles him, but at the same time part of him refuses to accept that the sphere is broken and worthless. He has picked up some of the fragments and stares at them intently in the hope that they will eventually bring him new knowledge.

I think of Laurence Arne-Sayles and an image rises up in my mind. It is the memory of a statue that stands in an upper vestibule, facing the head of a staircase (the one rising up out of the thirty-second vestibule). This statue represents a heretical pope seated on a throne. He is fat and bloated. He lolls on his throne, a shapeless mass. The throne is magnificent, but the sheer bulk of the figure threatens to split it in two. He knows that he is repulsive, but you can see by his face that the idea pleases him. He revels in the thought that he is somehow shocking. In his face there is mingled laughter and triumph. *Look at me*, he seems to say. *Look at me!*

I think of Raphael and an image – no, two images rise up in my mind.

In Piranesi's mind Raphael is represented by a statue in the forty-fourth western hall. It shows a queen in a chariot, the protector of her people. She is all goodness, all gentleness, all wisdom, all motherhood. That is Piranesi's view of Raphael, because Raphael saved him.

But I choose a different statue. In my mind Raphael is better represented by a statue in an antechamber that lies between the forty-fifth and the sixty-second northern halls. This statue shows a figure walking forward, holding a lantern. It is hard to determine with any certainty the gender of the figure; it is androgynous in appearance. From the way she (or he) holds up the lantern and peers at whatever is ahead, one gets the sense of a huge darkness surrounding her; above all I get the sense that she is alone, perhaps by choice or perhaps because no one else was courageous enough to follow her into the darkness.

Of all the billions of people in this world Raphael is the one I know best and love most. I understand much better now – better than Piranesi ever could – the magnificent thing she did in coming to find me, the magnitude of her courage.

I know that she returns to the labyrinth often. Sometimes we go together; sometimes she goes alone. The quiet and the solitude attract her strongly. In them she hopes to find what she needs.

It worries me.

'Don't disappear,' I tell her sternly. 'Do *not* disappear.'

She makes a rueful, amused face. 'I won't,' she says.

'We can't keep rescuing each other,' I say. 'It's ridiculous.'

She smiles. It is a smile with a little sadness in it.

But she still wears the perfume – the first thing I ever knew of her – and it still makes me think of Sunlight and Happiness.

In my mind are all the tides
ENTRY FOR 30 NOVEMBER 2018

In my mind are all the tides, their seasons, their ebbs and their flows. In my mind are all the halls, the endless procession of them, the intricate pathways. When this world becomes too much for me, when I grow tired of the noise and the dirt and the people, I close my eyes and I name a particular vestibule to myself; then I name a hall. I imagine I am walking the path from the vestibule to the hall. I note with precision the doors I must pass through, the rights and lefts that I must take, the statues on the walls that I must pass.

Last night I dreamt that I was standing in the fifth northern hall facing the statue of the gorilla. The gorilla dismounted from his plinth and came towards me with his slow knuckle-walk. He was grey-white in the moonlight; and I flung my arms around his massive neck and told him how happy I was to be home.

When I awoke I thought: *I am not home. I am here.*

It began to snow

This afternoon I walked through the city, making for a café where I was to meet Raphael. It was about half-past two on a day that had never really got light.

It began to snow. The low clouds made a grey ceiling for the city; the snow muffled the noise of the cars until it became almost rhythmical; a steady, shushing noise, like the sound of tides beating endlessly on marble walls.

I closed my eyes. I felt calm.

There was a park. I entered it and followed a path through an avenue of tall, ancient trees with wide, dusky, grassy spaces on either side of them. The pale snow sifted down through bare winter branches. The lights of the cars on the distant road sparkled through the trees: red, yellow, white. It was very quiet. Though it was not yet twilight the streetlights shed a faint light.

People were walking up and down on the path. An old man passed me. He looked sad and tired. He had broken veins on his cheeks and a bristly white beard. As he screwed up his eyes against the falling snow, I realised I knew him. He is depicted on the northern wall of the forty-eighth western hall. He is shown as a king with a little model of a walled city in one hand while the other hand he raises in blessing. I wanted to seize hold of him and say to him: *In another world you are a king, noble and good! I have seen it!* But I hesitated a moment too long and he disappeared into the crowd.

A woman passed me with two children. One of the children had a wooden recorder in his hands. I knew them too. They are depicted in the twenty-seventh southern hall: a statue of two children laughing, one of them holding a flute.

I came out of the park. The city streets rose up around me. There was a hotel with a courtyard with metal tables and chairs for people to sit in more clement weather. Today they were snow-strewn and forlorn. A lattice of wire was strung across the courtyard. Paper lanterns were hanging from the wires, spheres of vivid orange that blew and trembled in the snow and the thin wind; the sea-grey clouds raced across the sky and the orange lanterns shivered against them.

The Beauty of the House is immeasurable; its Kindness infinite.

A NOTE ON THE TYPE

The text of this book is set in Perpetua. This typeface is an adaptation of a style of letter that had been popularised for monumental work in stone by Eric Gill. Large scale drawings by Gill were given to Charles Malin, a Parisian punch-cutter, and his hand-cut punches were the basis for the font issued by Monotype. First used in a private translation called 'The Passion of Perpetua and Felicity', the italic was originally called Felicity.

ALSO AVAILABLE BY SUSANNA CLARKE

JONATHAN STRANGE & MR NORRELL

'Unquestionably the finest English novel of the fantastic written
in the last seventy years'
NEIL GAIMAN

The year is 1806. Centuries have passed since practical magicians faded into
the nation's past. But scholars of this glorious history discover that one remains:
the reclusive Mr Norrell, whose displays of magic send a thrill through the
country. Proceeding to London, he raises a beautiful woman from the dead and
summons an army of ghostly ships to terrify the French. Yet the cautious,
fussy Norrell is challenged by the emergence of another magician: the brilliant
novice Jonathan Strange. Young, handsome and daring, Strange is the very
antithesis of Norrell. So begins a dangerous battle between these two great
men which overwhelms that between England and France. And their own
obsessions and secret dabblings with the dark arts are going to cause more
trouble than they can imagine.

'Susanna Clarke perfectly conveys all that can be brilliant about
British literature'
GUARDIAN

'A highly original and compelling work'
SUNDAY TIMES

'Many books are to be read, some are to be studied, and a few are meant to be
lived in for weeks. *Jonathan Strange & Mr Norrell* is of this last kind'
WASHINGTON POST

ORDER YOUR COPY:

BY PHONE: +44 (0) 1256 302 699; **BY EMAIL:** DIRECT@MACMILLAN.CO.UK
DELIVERY IS USUALLY 3–5 WORKING DAYS. FREE POSTAGE AND PACKAGING FOR ORDERS OVER £20.
ONLINE: WWW.BLOOMSBURY.COM/BOOKSHOP
PRICES AND AVAILABILITY SUBJECT TO CHANGE WITHOUT NOTICE.

BLOOMSBURY.COM/AUTHOR/SUSANNA-CLARKE

BLOOMSBURY

THE LADIES OF GRACE ADIEU

A gorgeous book of stories from the world of *Jonathan Strange &*
Mr Norrell and illustrated by Charles Vess

Faerie is never as far away as you think. Sometimes you find you have crossed
an invisible line and must cope, as best you can, with petulant princesses, venge-
ful owls, ladies who pass their time embroidering terrible fates or with endless
paths in deep, dark woods and houses that never appear the same way twice.
The heroines and heroes bedevilled by such problems in these fairy tales include
a conceited Regency clergyman, an eighteenth-century Jewish doctor and Mary,
Queen of Scots, as well as two characters from *Jonathan Strange & Mr Norrell*:
Strange himself and the Raven King.

'An unholy alliance of Austen and Angela Carter'
DAILY MAIL

'These tales read as if Jane Austen had rewritten the Brothers Grimm'
SPECTATOR

'Witty rejoinders and genteel manners to contrast nicely with the darker tones
of hauntings, shape-changing and black magic ... Clarke is a natural storyteller'
SUNDAY TELEGRAPH

ORDER YOUR COPY:

BY PHONE: +44 (0) 1256 302 699; **BY EMAIL:** DIRECT@MACMILLAN.CO.UK
DELIVERY IS USUALLY 3–5 WORKING DAYS. FREE POSTAGE AND PACKAGING FOR ORDERS OVER £20.
ONLINE: WWW.BLOOMSBURY.COM/BOOKSHOP
PRICES AND AVAILABILITY SUBJECT TO CHANGE WITHOUT NOTICE.

BLOOMSBURY.COM/AUTHOR/SUSANNA-CLARKE

BLOOMSBURY